I0744092

Hot SPELL

Sweet Escape Series – Book Two

MIA LONDON & SUSAN SHEEHEY

AMEPPHIRE PRESS

Hot Spell
Sweet Escape Series
Book Two
by Mia London and Susan Sheehey

This is a work of fiction. Names, characters, places and incidents either are the product of the author's imagination or are used factitiously, and any resemblance to actual persons, living or dead, business establishments, event or locales is entirely coincidental.

ISBN: 978-1947874114 (E-Book)
978-1947874145 (paperback)

Publisher: Amepphire Press
11923 NE Sumner St, Ste 766015
Portland, OR 97220

Edited by Traci Hall
Formatted by Formatting by Leigh
Cover design copyright © L.J. Anderson, Mayhem Cover Creations

Published in the United States of America

Dedication

To ladies' trips and weekends.
The saviors of countless sanities and lives
everywhere.
We raise our wine glasses to you.

Life To The Max
Wanton Angel *(Prequel to Life To The Max)*

Beyond Lace (Hard Men of the Rockies 4)

Other Novels by Susan Sheehey

Royals of Solana Series
Prince of Solana

Jewel of Solana

Crown of Solana

Royal Wedding novella

Knights of Texas Series
Tell Me What You Want

Tell Me What You Crave

Tell Me What You Need

Tell Me What You Feel

Audrey's Promise

Chapter ONE

JORDAN WINCED AS Liddy grabbed the mini snow globe off the dresser—the one Frank had bought her on their lovers' getaway to San Diego—and threw it at the wall. The trinket shattered into a million pieces and tiny shrapnel flew halfway across the room.

"Ugh!" her friend bellowed, and slumped down on the end of her bed. "What a prick!" Soon the huffs of anger turned to sobs.

Jordan grabbed tissue box off Liddy's nightstand before the snot from her nose dropped onto the carpet. "Here." She handed a fresh tissue to her friend. "That snow globe didn't go with the rest your collection anyway."

Tears streamed down Liddy's cheeks from her red, swollen eyes. She looked like hell. "I just can't believe it." *Blow. Sniffle.* "I really thought he was the one."

Jordan glanced at Sam to see her eyes roll. Translation, *how many times have we heard that line?*

Sam rubbed her back. "I know."

Blow. Sniffle.

"Things were going so well between us," Liddy choked out.

Well, it appears not. Jordan didn't mean to be cold, but how many of Liddy's breakups had they endured?

Lydia Michelle Drake was a sweetheart. Truly kind and fun-loving, but clingy as shit. After a few months—sometimes weeks—men caught whiff of her clinginess and high-tailed it out of there. Kudos to Frank for lasting six months.

"Sweetie, do you want some hot tea?" Jordan asked.

"Sure." *Sniffle. Blow.*

"Sam, give me a hand, would ya?"

Samantha followed her into the kitchen, and they started their routine of making tea. They'd pulled this ritual often enough, they knew where everything was.

"It's different this time, Jordan," Sam observed. "She's taking it a lot harder."

"I know. Probably because Frank stayed with her for so long," Jordan whispered back.

"We gotta fix this."

"Hell, if I know what to do," she replied as she dug out the creamer.

They worked side-by-side in silence. Sam found scones and set them on a platter. Jordan brought down plates and cups from the cabinet.

"I got it," Sam said with a smile on her lips.

"What?"

"A vacation."

Jordan tapped her lips, the gears grinding in her mind.

"Let's go somewhere. Get her the hell out of here. Change of scenery and all that."

"Yeah, that could work." The words came out slowly. "It's been almost a year since our last vacation."

"Yup. Worked wonders for me. Got me out of my funk."

"Not that you would admit it at the time," Jordan said with a grin.

"Okay, Miss Priceline, go work your magic. Find us a good deal to go somewhere."

"Where are you thinking, Florida? Or New York for a girl's weekend?"

Sam hesitated. "No, I think we need farther. Like, out of the country."

Jordan nodded. The thoughts already brewed on high steam.

JORDAN HAD A mission as she booted up her computer: find a fix for Liddy's broken heart. A good distraction could help her sweet, naive friend realize she and Frank weren't meant to be forever.

Speaking of which, when was her last, er, distraction? This vacation could be good for her, too.

The usual column of ads populated the right side of her screen. She immediately went to her favorite discount vacation site. A few images of Mexican beaches quickly popped up. She typed in the search bar.

I wonder if Europe is on sale this time of year.

She scrolled down the page. Way too many zeros involved. *Okay, perhaps we won't be going* that *far away.*

Maybe Australia. *Wait, isn't it winter there now?*

She opened another site—more ads for Mexico.

"All right, all right," she told the computer.

She clicked on the various deals: Cozumel, Cancun, *oh,* Puerto Vallarta. *Now isn't that a great looking resort?* The all-inclusive property shaped in a big U was situated right on the ocean. They flouted a private beach, several pools, bars and restaurants, a nightclub, spa packages, and shuttle service from the airport.

"Puerto Vallarta it is," she said to no one.

She'd been to Mexico a few times; it was a relatively easy trip from San Francisco. Never been to Puerto Vallarta.

Although she could see the Latin in her dark brown eyes, olive skin, and brown wavy hair every time she looked in the mirror—she didn't speak Spanish fluently. All the Latin blood came down from her father's side. Retired military, her dad had instilled his intense work ethic in Jordan at an early age.

School was out for the summer, and her coaching duties for high school cheerleading camp weren't for another six weeks. Sam ran her own online software firm, and could manage it from anywhere, even across international borders.

The only real question was Liddy. Could she get the time

off from her retail job? Would she even try, with how reclusive she tended to be after a breakup?

Jordan glanced across the room, at her various gymnastics trophies and plaques. The bronze medal dangled from the arm of one trophy, from the Olympic trials her senior year in high school. She'd missed her final vault, and lost her spot on the official team . . . by three tenths of a point.

She stood, stretched out her muscles and touched the floor, keeping her legs straight. Her ACL protested. It was an old injury, but sitting too long exacerbated it.

She picked up her phone and shot a text to Sam.

Get your passport. Puerto Vallarta awaits.

Sam replied quickly. *Ole!*

Jordan smiled and dialed Liddy's number.

"Hello?" Her friend sighed, so depressed in her quiet, monotone voice.

"Hey sweetie. How are you doing today?"

Another sigh, longer than the first. "I'm alright."

Not likely. "Well, you will be. Let's get away. I found a great deal for us at an all-inclusive resort. We leave next week."

"Oh, I remember you guys talked about it, but I don't know, Jordan . . ."

"Baby, you sound like crap, which means you feel like crap, which means your work is like crap." She exhaled. "Ask your boss. I bet Bernie would be thrilled to have you take a week off. C'mon, it'll be good."

"I'll ask, but don't book anything until I know for sure."

"Call me back."

They disconnected and before Jordan could get back from her kitchen with a green smoothie, Liddy replied.

I can't believe it. He said take as much time as I need.

"That's my girl." Jordan spun in her seat to face her screen. "Beautiful Mexico, here we come."

Chapter TWO

THE SALTY OCEAN air was like an aggressive kiss on Jordan's cheeks as she stepped off the shuttle after a brief ride from the airport. The strong breeze sent her long hair whipping across her face. The heat and humidity embraced her in a friendly warning.

Trouble ahead, but you'll love every second.

"Damn, girl." Sam stepped out on the other side, lifting her oversized sunglasses onto her head, and stared at the resort. "You sure can pick 'em. Who'd you have to sleep with to get a deal on this place?"

"No one. Just had to pay a hacker a year's supply of Hot Pockets."

Liddy, super quiet during the three-and-a-half-hour flight, climbed down, her skin a little pale behind her thin-rimmed rose sunglasses. She clutched her Prada tote against her chest. "What hacker?"

Jordan shook her head. "It was a joke, sweetie. Come on. Paradise awaits."

They tipped the shuttle driver, and checked in at the front desk. Room keys in hand, they followed the bellboy to their rooms on the other side of the resort.

The open lobby gave the girls a great view of the grand pool area that stretched right up to the beach.

"Wow," Sam breathed out.

Chaise lounges surrounded the massive, W-shaped pool, some in the sun and others under thatch-roof canopies. In the shallow end, fathers tossed their kids from their shoulders, while mothers snapped pictures and laughed. Toward the deeper ends, more guests soaked up the sun reclining on clear inflatable chairs.

The hint of a smile crossed Liddy's face as she took in the spectacular view.

Jordan had a good feeling about this vacation. *There's still hope in our girl, yet.*

THE SUITE WAS even better than the online photos. Crisp white linens decorated the two queen beds with colorful accents of orange, purple, and green. Four sofa pillows positioned together created an abstract plumeria flower, each corner of the pillow making up a petal. Creative and charming—which made Jordan happy since online booking was often a crap-shoot, especially with a hotel not part of a chain.

The main room held a kitchenette, counter with ergonomic cream stools, a coffee table in front of the sleeper-sofa, and a dresser doubling as a TV stand.

All paled in comparison to the view outside the wide, double-door balcony.

Beyond the sheer curtains fluttering in the breeze lay the glorious, glittering ocean. The afternoon sun shimmered off the water, the reflection creating a haze on the horizon.

The beach called to her. Seagulls cawing, jet skis whipping by, and the constant rushing waves . . . her new soundtrack on life.

At least for the week.

"Okay, ladies. You know the rules. Bikinis, sunblock, and beach. *Pronto*," Jordan announced as she heaved her rolling suitcase onto the hotel's luggage rack. "Time to break in the new batch of cabana boys."

She'd finished texting her loving, yet overbearing father that they'd arrived safely. If she hadn't, then he'd probably send in a search party using his old commando buddies.

"What about touring the hotel?" Liddy protested. Finally, the woman had stopped crying and sniffling, and even a little pink had returned to her cheeks. The Mexican ambiance was already working, pulling her out of her funk.

"We'll have time for that later. Warm sunshine is just what Dr. Beck orders."

"I wouldn't argue with her," Sam murmured as she passed Liddy on the way to the bathroom, suit in hand.

"Fine," Liddy pouted and unpacked her bag, shoving clothes into dresser drawers.

As Jordan rummaged through her bag to retrieve her bathing suit and flip-flops, the sight of Sam on her phone caught her eye.

"Samantha Louise Callahan. For the love of margaritas, you better put down that phone." She used her most commanding voice, so effortlessly attained.

Sam grinned at the screen. "Chase wanted to know if we arrived safely." She snorted at something she read, and typed a response. "He said if I'm going to the beach, I need to wear the moo-moo."

Liddy chuckled from the bathroom.

Jordan smiled. "Fine. Bring the detestable thing with you. We'll take a picture, send it to him, then burn it. We're here to find a nice distraction for Liddy, and you're our bait."

"Um, little problem," Sam replied, flashing her one-carat solitaire engagement ring.

"I know. I promise we won't get you in too much trouble. You'll reel in the prospects, while Liddy and I do the nibbling."

Truly, she adored Chase, and loved how great those two were together. Everyone was thrilled. They hadn't set a date yet, but Sam claimed they'd wait until Chase's ASD living center was up and running.

Jordan slid her dark sunglasses on the top of her head, and picked up her ball cap and cover-up. She'd bought a new suit for the occasion—a red, athletic-cut bikini, trimmed in white, with a zipper clasping her B-cup boobs in place.

Sam grabbed her beach bag and threw her sunblock inside. As promised, she wore the navy moo-moo. Jordan was slightly envious of the Scarlet Johansson curves underneath Sam's cover-up, which is what they'd use to lure in Liddy's eye-candy.

Liddy stepped out of the bathroom, wearing simple denim shorts and a tank top over the green bathing suit from last year. "Okay, I guess I'm ready."

Walking off the elevator, the trio headed toward the lobby and out to the pool area. The afternoon sun was bright, and the island music playing through the surround-sound speakers gave Jordan a little kick of adrenaline.

A handful of white-uniformed wait staff meandered about the pool deck, taking food and drink orders. At the center of the pool a swim-up bar was perfectly positioned to serve anyone in the chilled water. Frozen drink machines whirred to life with daiquiris including cliché paper umbrellas poised on the rim. Clearly, this is where the younger adult crowd hung out. All in suits, oiled up, ready to flirt.

This was everything Jordan had been looking for. If they couldn't find a vacation fling for their friend here, they had no right to call themselves red-blooded American women.

As they made their way to the beach, Jordan's gaze stopped on one of the bartenders. A tall, dark-haired man with a nice tan and sculpted arms. She couldn't see his entire frame—just enough to know she wanted to see more.

He looked up and spotted her passing by.

Wow! A pair of beautiful emerald green eyes looked up at her. His lip curved at the corner, and if she wasn't wearing her dark sunglasses, she would've sent him a wink.

A little fling for myself can't hurt.

It was late afternoon when they arrived at the sandy beach and were lucky to get a thatch-covered cabana vacated by a family of four leaving early for dinner.

Jordan didn't hesitate. She flung off her hat and glasses, stripped off her clothes, and bolted for the water—eager to rinse off California, responsibilities, and adult behavior.

Chapter THREE

SHOULD WE STICK with our traditional vacation drink, screaming orgasms, or shake things up?" Sam strolled over to the walk-up bar in the pool. The first hour by the ocean had drained their inhibitions, and now they needed a drink.

"Let's make this trip official. I'm all about the gaudy frozen cocktails with obscene names." Jordan raised her hand at the bartender.

"Hell, yeah." Liddy gave a slow nod.

A brown-haired man turned around from helping another group of ladies on the far side.

Jordan nearly dropped her room key.

Piercing green eyes met her stare head-on. The perfectly symmetrical smile matched the perfectly tanned skin. Jordan managed a quick glance at his muscular frame before his American accent pulled her focus back to his face.

"The California sirens! Call me one lucky man."

Liddy eyed him. "How'd you know we were from Cali?"

"Lucky guess. Your 49ers cap." He motioned with a jerk of his chin toward her head.

Jordan subconsciously ran a hand over her hat and ponytail, and smirked. "Aren't you observant," she read his name tag, "Zac." The same man who'd caught her attention when they first arrived. "Well, Zac. I'm Jordan. This is Sam and Liddy," she gestured with her hand. "If you're worth your salt, tell us what most San Francisco gals want to drink."

Zac rested his elbows on the bar, and leaned forward. "I'm smart enough to know *never* tell a woman what she wants to drink. But if she *asks,*" he straightened again, "you can never go wrong with my mango margarita."

This guy's gonna be fun.

"We'll take three," she cooed.

As Zac went to work on their drinks, he asked, "What brings you all to paradise?"

Liddy pulled her sunglasses off her face. "Just a break."

"Actually," Sam cut in, "we need to find Liddy here a fling."

Liddy gasped, and glared at Sam.

Zac didn't even pause. "That's what vacations are for." He grinned.

"We could use some help," Jordan added. "A little reconnaissance. Notice any decent contenders?"

He chuckled, and a small tinge of pink graced his cheeks. "What's her type?"

"Human," Sam laughed. "Male."

Liddy smacked her shoulder.

"English speaking?" he asked.

"Yes," Liddy answered.

"At least a little," Sam interjected. "Just enough to get the meaning across."

Zac's smirk widened. He nodded over to a group by the volleyball net. "That group arrived two days ago, from Canada."

Jordan discreetly turned her head. The four men wore shirts over their bare chests as they played. "What's with the cover-ups?"

"Pale skin and the Mexican sun don't mix." He poured margaritas into their glasses, and garnished the rims with mango slices. "Vicious sunburns, all of them."

Liddy winced. "I'm not so sure."

"Yeah." Jordan slipped the mango garnish between her teeth. "She likes to cuddle, so definitely not the second-degree burners."

"How about that one from Miami?" He gestured to the man strolling up from the beach. "Has cash coming out of his . . ."

Said man was easily three hundred pounds, and sported a bright green banana hammock. Sun glinted off the gold wrist watch and necklace.

"Not so sure that'll be worth it." Sam put her sunglasses back on to hide her wide eyes.

Jordan laughed. "You were always a fan of whale

watching."

This time, Zac laughed. "This first round is on me, ladies."

"I'd be flattered, except it's all-inclusive. Nice try." The first generous sip of fruity alcohol went straight to her brain.

"Ooh, that's *good*." Liddy drank more, and waved her thanks to the bartender, then retreated to their cabana. Sam followed.

Jordan hung back. "You're American."

"What gave it away?"

She twirled the straw in her drink. "What brought you down here?"

The man wore a perpetual smile as he wiped up the counter. "Came down here for spring break in college, and never left."

She tilted her head. "You've used that line a bit, haven't you?"

He tucked the towel into his black apron. "Didn't fall for it?"

Jordan shook her head. "Too canned."

The way the man smiled made her feel hotter than the sand. Zac was average height, average build, but she hadn't met many guys with a smile like that.

The other bartender had been juggling liquor bottles and called Zac's name as he finished his show.

"Enjoy the drink. I'm here if you need more." He winked before moving to the other side of the bar.

She returned to the cabana, drinking slowly so the strong concoction would last longer—Jordan didn't want to lose her head too quickly. She pulled back the curtain on one side to watch Zac.

The man easily controlled his surroundings, entertaining and yet expert at serving his guests. She didn't have to wait long to see he was just as capable of flipping around the liquor bottles as his friend, but he didn't feel the need to show off.

More natural and laid-back.

Even when two slightly burly men started having words with each other in the pool, Zac easily diffused the situation by cracking a few jokes before the security guards arrived.

"You've been super quiet," Sam interrupted her thoughts.

"Just takin' it all in," she replied with a smile.

Sam turned to the object of Jordan's attention. Zac. "You like the bartender?"

The question didn't require an answer, but she did nonetheless. "You know it."

Liddy finished taking another selfie—her mood clearly improving— and glanced in their direction. "He's super cute."

"You think he's your fling?" Jordan returned a reserved smile. As much as she wanted Zac to be her own Mexican distraction, this trip was about Liddy. If her friend thought Zac was the right contender, the choice was simple.

Liddy's forehead creased as she stared at the bartender.

"Nah. Reminds me too much of my foster brother. But you totally should."

The little devil on Jordan's shoulder started dancing for joy. "Let's snap a few shots with us together and send them to Chase so Sam doesn't have to carry the phone around with her the rest of the trip."

"Down by the beach so we get the ocean behind us." Sam grabbed her phone.

They corralled together in front of the surf, Jordan holding the camera. She waited just until the parasailer was in the shot behind them, then snapped the picture.

Sam texted the photo to her fiancé, as well as Jordan and Liddy—it was one of their best images they'd ever taken.

Jordan was sure that keeper would sit on her nightstand for years to come.

"I'm bringing my sexy back," someone yelled from the pool bar.

Jordan turned to see the commotion.

A group of ladies laughed by the counter, clearly a girl's trip, like theirs. Zac and another bartender passed them their drinks, though the shorter woman with a black braid swayed unsteadily. She leaned on one of the stools, singing off-key to some song.

"We might have some competition," Jordan laughed. "Those women already have their buzz going, strong and loud."

The drunk woman reached across the bar and stroked

the other bartender's face. His smile widened as he focused all his attention on her.

"He'll be getting a big tip, that's for sure," Sam muttered. "Now, time to show off. Jordan..."

"What, here?"

"I know you still have the moves. Show everyone—especially Zac—how *flexible* you are."

"On uneven sand. You're asking me to put my body in harm's way for your own amusement? And potential for attracting guys?"

"And the previous times you've done exactly that on other beach vacations were different how?"

Jordan scratched her head, pretending to think. "You got me there. Still, God doesn't like a bragger."

"I dare you."

Jordan smirked. That's all it ever took for her friends to get her to do something. Because Jordan Beck would never back down from a dare.

Chapter FOUR

ZAC WOULD HAVE to be blind not to notice Jordan's flips and handstands on the beach. Not to mention, how damn gorgeous that woman was in a bikini. It wasn't fair to mankind to have a body that built—it was so distracting, he'd never get anything done.

"Heads up," Simon called from the other side of the bar.

Zac blinked, and finally registered the elderly couple standing in front of him, requesting mai tais.

As he worked on them, he kept glancing back at the beach, at the cluster of women from San Francisco. Jordan's gymnastics had drawn a small crowd.

Her moves were impressive, especially since she performed them on sand rather than a gym mat. Every bend, dip and tuck were carefully placed and balanced. The sun shimmered off her skin. She finished a series of twirls into the splits, and he outwardly groaned.

A woman with muscles like that intimidated him. Teased him. Had him hooked.

"You don't see a woman like that every day," the elderly man said.

Zac nodded. "Absolutely not."

The man's wife smiled. "To be that young again. I remember when I used to pull in crowds like that from tap dancing."

"You don't need a crowd," Zac replied. "Just the right one. And it looks like you found yours." He placed their drinks on the counter.

The pair chuckled. "Bless you, young man."

They tipped him and left.

He gripped the cash. For the last five years, all his money had gone into the account to pay for his grandmother's treatments. Every dime had been worth it. He'd held his grandmother's hand in that hospital chair, as he read her favorite novels out loud. All romances with happy endings. She'd often recite those words to him at the end of each story. *You don't need scores of women, Zac, just the right one. I found my love in Ernesto, God bless his soul. You'll find yours, too.*

He finished cleaning up his station, his shift almost through for the day. He ducked under the counter to empty the trash.

A long, slow whistle came from behind him. Definitely Simon's whistle.

"It's Wonder Woman!"

Zac's head shot up.

Jordan and her friends approached the bar, all sweaty and smiling.

"Water," Jordan panted. "For the love of God, water."

He dropped the bag, filled a glass with ice, not bothering to use the scooper, and then added water.

Jordan downed the whole thing. "This heat really zaps your energy."

Zac filled it up again. "Yeah, the *heat*. Not the flips and cartwheels."

"My girl has mad skills," the honey blonde chimed in. "She almost went to the Olympics."

"Damn." *Intimidation factor increased ten-fold.*

"See any more prospects for Liddy here?" Jordan asked, downing her second glass of water.

Liddy climbed onto a stool. "I spotted a few down by the beach." She pointed at two guys with ripped abs over by the jet skis. "They seem right up my alley."

Zac had to fight off a laugh. "Do you mean gay?"

Her eyes widened. "No! Seriously?" She looked again. "No, they're not."

"Oh, yes they are. They were in the pool most of the morning. Lots of oil rubbing."

"Damn," she muttered, then readjusted her bikini top. "My whole radar is off."

Jordan patted her shoulder. "You've been singularly focused the last six months. But that's what you've got us for."

"How about you two?" Zac asked. "Should we find some

companions for you?"

"Sam's engaged. All she can do is look and drool."

The blonde flashed a brilliant diamond ring on her finger.

"That's a keeper," he replied. Maybe one day he'd be buying one of those. One day...way down the road.

"He sure is." Sam beamed.

"And for you, Miss Olympian?"

Jordan leaned on the bar, and looked him straight in the eye. "I need someone who can keep up with me."

Zac grinned through Sam's laughter. "Sounds like a fun challenge."

"She means it," her friend interrupted. "We're going hiking, followed by drinking, more beach time, and dancing. And that's just tomorrow."

Sweat dripped down Jordan's neck, a slow trail along her skin and landed in her cleavage. Her eyes filled with mischief and determination. Real *life*.

"If you see anyone who fits that description, Zac..." Jordan grabbed a cherry from the garnish tray, and stuck it between her teeth. Sucking the bright red fruit into her mouth, she left only the stem between her fingers. "Let me know." She winked. Then turned, and took a running dive into the pool. Like she was born doing it.

She certainly knows how to leave a man wanting.

THE LADIES STROLLED into their suite at a quarter

past one in the morning. Their sandals dangled from their fingers. The music still blared from the disco on the first floor, the bass reverberating in the air felt even from their suite on the fifth floor. The lights in the palm trees around the resort made Jordan feel like she'd entered heaven.

"I could see why someone moves here permanently." Sam sighed through a drunken reverie. "The beach really does have healing qualities for the soul." She tossed her shoes by the closet, and retreated into the bedroom to collapse on the bed. "That's why Chase's Santa Cruz house is so convenient."

"It's convenient because of the company," Jordan called and filled a glass with water from the kitchen.

"Their DJ is really good." Liddy stretched her arms above her head, standing on the patio with the sliding glass doors open to let in the breeze. "Some pretty decent prospects on that floor tonight. I liked the blond firefighter from Jersey."

One of the many her friend had danced with after dinner, but Jordan wasn't sure Liddy was sober enough to remember most of them.

"Make sure you all hydrate before you sleep. We have a big morning ahead."

Sam groaned from the mattress through the open door. "You and your excursions. You pulled the same crap in Santa Cruz."

Jordan came back to the bedroom with her glass of

water. "It'll be good for us."

"How many times do I have to say it? Vacations mean sleeping in." Sam pulled the pillow into the crook of her arm, cuddling it like a teddy bear, not bothering to change from her cut-off shorts and halter top to pajamas.

"We have plenty of time to sleep when we're dead."

"That's your father talking. I distinctly remember you sleeping in when you were hungover."

Jordan smirked. "We're going shopping afterward again."

Liddy laughed, her drunken smile following Jordan into the bedroom. Then subsequently collapsed on the other queen bed. "She knows us so well."

"The best part of heaven." She grinned.

"The *second* best part of heaven," Sam corrected.

"What's the first?"

Sam opened one eye, lazily looking at her from the side. "You girls."

Chapter FIVE

SAM, YOU'RE CLOSEST. Would you please come over here and pluck this stray?" Jordan leaned over the sink, staring five inches from the mirror. Why did she have to have so much Latin blood? She plucked, tweezed, shaved, and waxed constantly to keep the body hair under control.

"What stray?" Sam stepped next to Jordan.

Jordan held her index finger under her right eyebrow. "That sucker."

"Oh, for goodness sake. That thing is barely out an eighth of an inch." She took the tweezers and made a pass at the offending hair. Sam tried several more times.

"Any luck?' Jordan stood patiently.

"Jordan, you are such a perfectionist sometimes, I swear."

"Yes, she is," Liddy called from the main room.

"Am not."

"You are, babe, but we still love you." Sam returned the tweezers.

"Thank you."

Sam walked away wearing a smug smile, and Jordan knew her friend was a little right. At times she was a bit too picky. *Sometimes.*

She also knew where it came from—her father. Military bred, with Venezuelan blood. AKA, strict, severe, and unrelenting.

"Anyone seen my other hiking boot?" Liddy staggered out of the bedroom wearing only one new brown hiking boot, with her honey blonde hair in a messy bun atop her head.

Jordan poked her head out of the doorway. "Check in your suitcase."

"I'm ready," Sam announced.

Jordan pulled her ponytail through her ball cap. "We have ten minutes to make it down to the tour bus."

With time to actually plan a few events for this trip, Jordan had signed them up for a hike and lunch tour on the trails of the Sierra Madre Mountains. A healthy dose of nature was always good in fighting off depression and would help Liddy.

Zac's smile flashed in Jordan's mind; she couldn't help but wish he would join them on the hike. He had a quiet confidence that Jordan found vastly appealing. Coupled with his easy smile and green eyes, he was downright irresistible. But why would an American move to a resort in Mexico to be a bartender?

"I don't know how I feel about hiking," Liddy whined.

"This is supposed to be a vacation, not work. When do we get to 'hike' the beach?"

Jordan grinned. "If we're finished early enough, we can go to that outdoor shopping area, the Malecon, and shop. Remember, tonight is Throwback Thursday in the bar. We get to dance our asses off to the eighties."

"If I'm not too tired," Liddy joked.

AFTER SEVERAL HOURS of easy hiking, snapping a bunch of pictures, and eating from a Mexican buffet the tour guides had arranged, the ladies were far too tired for the Malecon. Well, mostly Sam and Liddy.

"Go rest for a while. Dinner and dancing start at seven."

"Yes, Mom." Liddy and Sam spoke in unison from the bedroom.

Jordan chuckled and pulled off her hiking boots. Streaks of dirt clung to her calves and ankles and she started washing them off in the shower.

Even after hiking, energy pulsed through her veins. She stripped out of her clothes into a swimsuit. Dinner wasn't for a few hours, so she'd swim a few laps in the pool.

Just maybe she'd run into Zac. She could casually ask him if he was going to be at the disco tonight.

She grinned and, beach bag in hand, headed to the pool.

She plopped her things on a chaise lounge, and glanced at the pool bar. There was no sign of Zac.

The circular bar was massive. Half served patrons in the pool, with stools nailed into the bottom so they could swim up and sit under a canopy. The other half served the patio off the pool deck, with an easy walk up from the beach.

The pool area was just as busy as the prior day. People in the pool, kids laughing, and several reclining under the cabanas, staying in the shade.

Jordan dove in the deep end. After a few laps—mostly freestyle and backstroke—working around a few others in the pool, there was still no sign of Zac.

She swam to the step, retrieved her towel and headed to the bar. The bartender on duty had black shiny hair, dark chocolate eyes, and dimples when he smiled. Mercy!

"Hi, I'm Marco. What can I get for you?" He had a slight Mexican accent.

"A rum punch, please. And . . . do you know if Zac is working?"

Marco mixed various liquors in a tumbler. "Not now, but he closes tonight. In the inside bar. It's Throwback Thursday. Tonight's tunes are Madonna and Gloria Estefan."

She signed the slip verifying her room number for the drinks. "Always up for some Gloria. Thanks, Marco."

"*De nada.* See you tonight."

"You, too." Drink in hand, she strolled back to their suite.

Her disappointment wasn't too great. Sure, she'd hoped to see Zac here, and flirt some more. But at least tonight held some serious promise. When the elevator doors closed, she muttered to her reflection, "Time to "Get On Your Feet," girls."

ZAC DURANT WALKED through the lobby for his shift, where the police were talking to a woman by the concierge. Tangles marred her long black braid, and tears streamed down her cheeks.

He approached Joaquin, the resort's divemaster, as he checked sign-ups for this evening's night dives. "What's going on over there?"

Joaquin scowled and shuffled the paperwork. "Another robbery. She claims she was too drunk to remember anything, but last night her whole room was ransacked."

"Damn. That's what . . . the fourth one this month?"

Joaquin shrugged. "Watch yourself. I think *el detective* believes it's an inside job."

"Really?"

"He's interviewed a bunch of employees already."

"Shit," Zac breathed out.

"Do you recognize her?" Joaquin tossed his pen in a drawer.

"She was at the bar yesterday. But so were a lot of people." Including a San Francisco gymnast he'd dreamt about last night.

"Well, they will surely talk to you at some point."

The police officer turned around, and Zac recognized him. Not an officer, but Detective Miguel Lacruz—a friend of his grandmother's.

"Hey," Joaquin tapped his shoulder. "I could use your help on Saturday. Already a full boat, and I'm a man short."

"Sure."

"If you still work here by then."

Zac frowned at him. "Not funny."

"*Hasta luego.*"

Zac arrived at the bar to see the Opener and Barback One already prepping. Since their stations served the restaurant, they'd be busy filling orders until the kitchen closed at eleven.

On Thursdays, the bar started getting packed when the DJ came on at nine. Zac scanned the bar several times for signs of Jordan or her friends. Surely, they would come to the bar that night. Everyone loved dancing to the eighties.

Zac, for one, would love to watch that gorgeous body and rockin' ass move on the dance floor. His mouth watered.

No sooner had the thought crossed his mind when the very object of his desire entered the bar.

Jordan wore a short, navy, body-hugging dress with strappy heel sandals. Her dark hair hung down her back in endless loose curls. As she came closer, Zac spotted a hot pink streak running down the side.

He smiled.

"Hi, Zac. You remember Liddy and Sam."

"Impossible to forget. Hi, ladies. How's my favorite California crew tonight?"

"Fabulous. Ready for some serious dancing." Her smile lit up the room, even brighter than the spinning glass ball dangling from the ceiling.

"How is the search going Liddy?"

"Slow, but I'm hopeful."

"So, what would fit the bill?"

"I think I need the full vacation experience. Hispanic, definitely speaks English, but can show me all the fun Puerto Vallarta has to offer. Give me a real escape."

"*Increíble*," Marco answered, and walked over. "You just described me." He flashed his toothy white grin.

Zac bit down on the inside of his cheek, trying to hold back a smirk.

"*Soy* Marco. How can I help make all your dreams come true?" He reached out his hand.

Liddy placed hers in his. Her dumbstruck look was one Zac had seen many times on other women his friend had charmed.

Marco kissed her knuckles.

The pair chatted away, Liddy falling for the Latino's enchantment like a teenager to a boy band rockstar.

"Well, that was easy," Jordan said under her breath.

"Maybe we can start off with some yummy drinks, Zac," Sam chimed in.

"Absolutely. Here's the list of drink specials for the

evening." He glanced to a group to the left, waiting. "I'll be right back."

He served the two guys and a woman a pitcher of margaritas, watching Jordan from the corner of his eye as she read the list aloud. "Alabama slammer, blue lagoon, fuzzy navel, B-52, Long Island iced tea, piña colada, Harvey Wallbanger, and Singapore sling."

"Ohmigosh. All the favorites from the eighties," Sam said with a grin.

"I haven't had a L.I.T. in forever. I'll take that," Liddy said.

"Me, too." Sam raised her hand.

"Okay," Jordan replied. "I'll order. How about you guys find a place to sit."

Zac immediately returned to Jordan. "What's the decision? Three Long Island iced teas?"

She tapped her fingers on the counter. "You hear everything, don't you? Yes, I'll take three."

Zac made the drinks, keeping an eye on his San Francisco flirt. "Here ya' go," he said, reaching below to pull up three cherry jelly shots, "to kick off your night." He set the drinks on a tray.

Her eyes flashed with glee. "You're offering me a cherry? Amen, I've been missing mine for quite some time."

Heat filled his face.

The corner of her lip curved upward as she grabbed the tray, and spun to meet her friends.

Women flirted with him all the time. That was part of the job, and he'd earned a lot of tips over the years. He wasn't bad looking, and when people were having a good time, he never felt guilty when they wanted to fill his pockets. But never once had he felt this strong of an urge to take it further.

Jordan was gorgeous, her smile seductive, and her laugh spellbinding. A true fireball that left him wanting ever since she'd set foot on his resort. With her, it didn't feel like the same run-of-the-mill flirtation. No, Jordan reached a whole 'nother level.

Chapter SIX

NOT SINCE SANTA Cruz, have I had this much fun." Jordan plopped into her chair and sucked on the straw of her second Long Island iced tea.

"Here, here," Liddy agreed.

The women panted from exertion.

"Damn, that man is a good mixologist," Sam said of Zac.

"Almost as good as yours, right?" Jordan stirred the nearly melted ice in her drink.

The women giggled.

"You know it." Sam nodded.

Liddy straightened in her chair. Two women chatted with the DJ as one of them handed him a napkin. He read it quickly and nodded. "Hey! It looks like the DJ takes requests."

Jordan twisted in her seat.

"Oh, that gives me a great idea." Jordan flashed a mischievous smile.

She rose and leaned over to the table next to them,

asking to borrow a pen. She scribbled one of her favorite Prince songs on the cocktail napkin and headed to the DJ.

"Any chance you can play this?" she asked over the music.

"*Perfecto.*"

"Do you ever see the bartenders get out here?"

"Yeah, occasionally."

"Thanks." She pivoted on her heel and bee-lined for the bar.

Zac was already grinning at her from ten paces off.

"Hey, pretty lady."

"Dance with me."

He lifted an eyebrow. "I'm working."

"Take a quick break. C'mon. One dance. My favorite song is coming up."

He scrubbed the scruff on his jaw. He really wanted to, that much was clear from the anticipation on his face. He glanced at the other two employees behind the bar, easily managing the patrons wanting to order.

The song ended, and the first few beats of her favorite song poured through the speakers. "Little Red Corvette."

The corner of his mouth lifted. He muttered something in the other bartender's ear, then came around the side, tossing his towel behind him.

Jordan's heart leapt to the ceiling. The second his hand slipped into hers, she melted.

His skin was rough, but warm, and his strong grip led

her to the floor.

The DJ pointed at them with a wink.

They danced to the fast beat, and she couldn't wipe the smile off her face. Zac grinned and spun her around a few times. He made the moves look so easy. His gaze stayed on hers like she was the only one in the room.

The DJ announced he'd play a slow song for everyone to catch their breaths, and when Zac glanced up at the DJ booth, the man winked at him as "Take My Breath Away" began to play over the speakers.

Jordan liked that DJ more and more. She took her cue, and stepped closer to him. Zac wrapped his arms around her for a slower pace. She slid her hands up his arms and clasped them around the back of his neck. He smelled like sugar and vodka.

"He's a sly one," Jordan noted.

The corner of Zac's mouth lifted. "Yes, he is."

After a beat, she asked, "You don't have a girlfriend, do you?"

"No. Why?"

"Because if I kiss you right now, I need to know who I'll have to contend with." *Please tell me he doesn't have a girlfriend.*

The corner of his mouth pulled up. "Well, you're free and clear. No jealous girlfriend waiting in the wings."

"Thank God."

"I happen to have a thing for tanned skin and packed

abs."

That was all the confirmation Jordan needed to hear. She pushed onto her toes and brought her lips to his, brushing against them softly. Then she closed any remaining gap between them. His lips parted, and tilted his head for more.

She pulled herself into him and took the kiss deeper, letting her eyelids drift closed. The sugary scent matched his taste, savory and addicting.

He kissed like a dream.

Her tongue danced with his, matching his eager energy. He squeezed her tight one last time before releasing her.

She opened her eyes to see him smiling.

"Damn." He made a quick glance toward the bar. "That's the kind of kiss that could get me fired."

She blushed. Actually blushed. Men rarely made Jordan blush, but she could feel it from her chest, creeping all the way up her face.

"Zac, I know you're working late tonight. What about tomorrow?"

"I work until eleven."

"Let's do something after you're off. Go for a drive or something."

He paused for a moment, contemplating. "Okay. Tomorrow. Meet me by the lobby."

She smiled, and after the dance he led her off the floor back to her table. "Thanks for the dance." He gave her a wink before heading back behind the bar.

Sam's indulgent smile told her she'd witnessed the whole thing. "Good?"

"Hell yeah." She fanned herself, and stole one last look at her bartender. "We're going out tomorrow after he gets off work."

"Good for you."

"By the way, where's Liddy?"

Sam motioned with her chin toward the dancefloor.

Jordan twisted in her seat to see Liddy and Marco dancing to the next song, something fast by Michael Jackson. Her hands were all over the guy. Clearly, enjoying herself. *Good for her.*

Jordan lifted her glass. "To perfect vacations."

Sam joined in with a smile. "Here. Here."

Chapter SEVEN

DETECTIVE LACRUZ FLICKED the lid of his coffee cup, the grimace on his weathered face filling the resort manager's office with a thick layer of tension.

"I'm sorry about this," he began, his voice hoarse from years of cigarettes and stale coffee. "But I have to interview the entire staff who were on the clock Wednesday."

"I understand, Miguel. I'll give you what I know." Zac had come in early for his shift at the manager's request. He already knew why.

"Do you remember the woman?"

The whole scenario bubbled in his stomach like rancid coffee. "She and a few friends came up to the pool bar in the afternoon, ordered mai tais. She was pretty hammered already."

"What time was that?"

"My shift started at three. So, around four, I'd say. She finished her drink by the pool, and then left with her friends. Twenty minutes, tops. I never saw her after that."

"Did you make her drink?"

"Simon and I teamed up. They ordered five drinks between them; the room charge will verify that."

"Simon was working with you?"

"Yeah, but I honestly can't remember who made which drink. I garnished all of them, I remember that."

Miguel wrote in his notepad.

"You seriously think this was an inside job?" Zac asked.

"Looks like it, with the string of robberies over the last six weeks. All the same MO. The assailant clearly knows where all the cameras are, so they've avoided getting recorded."

"Shit."

"Anyone look or act strangely to you?"

He shook his head. "I don't know Simon that well. He just started here two months ago."

Miguel scribbled more notes. "Any other employees come by the bar during your shift?"

Zac thought. "Marco came by to pick up his sunglasses he'd left the day before. But he didn't stay to work or anything."

"How long has Marco been with the resort?"

"About six months, though I've known him a good year. He's the nephew of my grandmother's oncologist."

Miguel's forehead creased. "How's she doing? Your grandmother?"

A small weight lifted off Zac's heart. "Next month is one

year in remission. She says she feels great. Even getting out to her garden more often."

Miguel smiled. "I'm happy to hear that. Tell her I'll be by with some *marronitos* in a few days. Those still her favorite?"

"Of course. But only a few. The doctor doesn't want her having that much sugar."

"Listen," the detective shifted in his seat. "I don't want to get you involved in this, because I owe your grandmother a lot. She paid my tuition for the police academy, and she and my mother go way back. But I don't have a choice. I have to follow procedure, and you were working during the shift when the woman was drugged."

Zac blinked. "She was drugged?"

The detective nodded. "So, I need to know your whereabouts the rest of the day after your shift. Through midnight at least."

He shook his head in disbelief. As he relayed everywhere he'd been Wednesday, he couldn't fathom someone getting roofied right under his nose.

What if it happened in front of me, and I missed it? How could I have missed it?

Even worse, what if Simon did it? Or tried to frame one of them for it?

"I'll check out your story, and let you know if I have more questions. But I really need you to keep your eyes open for me."

"Sure." Zac's stomach twisted at the thought of one of his friends mixed up in this.

"And Zac?" Miguel added.

He looked up.

"Keep your head down. Don't let anyone think you're a rat. Do you understand me?"

With a deep sigh, he nodded again. This was Mexico. He knew exactly what that meant. The cartel might be involved in this. Until they knew for certain, he had to assume this was the cartel.

Which meant things could get pretty damn dangerous.

"Shit," he breathed. "So much for fun in paradise."

JORDAN SIDESTEPPED AROUND a kid racing to grab his soccer ball in the middle of the busy Malecon shopping strip. The open-air walkway reminded her of the boardwalk in Santa Cruz, lined with palm trees and charming storefronts, but this was much bigger. The seaside attraction smelled of the ocean and fried plantains. Street artists displayed their work on concrete patios, and restaurant hosts called for patrons to enter and enjoy their specials.

"Ooh, look at those earrings." Liddy approached a vendor with jewelry displays, mostly silver, some shells, and mother-of-pearl hoops. Sam perused the necklaces, holding onto her sunhat to keep the breeze from blowing it away.

Jordan's cotton skirt furled around her brown shopping bag. She'd bought a Christmas ornament for her mother, but her father was much more difficult to buy for.

The next stall displayed hats of different kinds, jiggling in the breeze—including golf hats.

Maybe he'd like one of those.

She surveyed the choices, until her gaze landed on a straw fedora with a black ribbon around the brim. She smiled, removed her 49ers ball cap, and tried it on.

The mirror's reflection reminded her of a Cosmo picture with her favorite actress wearing a similar hat. This one fit perfectly.

"*Cuanto cuesta?*" she asked.

She paid in *pesos,* and shoved her ball cap in the bag.

Jordan looked up as a man stopped a soccer ball from rolling into the street, then returned it to the same kid she'd sidestepped earlier.

She squinted against the sun. One of the bartenders from the resort? *That looks like Marco.*

He laughed, waved to the kid's mom, and continued strolling down the Malecon. He was too far away for Jordan to wave or call out his name, but that was definitely the hot guy Liddy danced with the prior night.

"That's a gorgeous hat!" Liddy came up beside her. "You look like Mila Kunis."

She wiggled her eyebrows, and they moved down a few vendors. Sam purchased decorative plates and a bracelet, and Liddy bought a new purple beach wrap.

They found a quaint patio restaurant for lunch, the

sizzling fajitas that filled the air too mouthwatering to resist. They paired the meal with a margarita on the rocks, and then desperately needed to walk off the food.

On the beach, people carved large, elaborate sand castles, including a giant seashell as tall as Sam, who took several photos and posted on social media.

"Oh, look, Sam. A lighthouse." Jordan smirked.

Liddy burst out laughing. "Too bad Chase isn't here."

"I should never have told you that." Sam's cheeks flushed red.

"No, you shouldn't have," Jordan faked a wince. "Now, that's all I can think about when I see a lighthouse."

They laughed down the street a few more blocks.

"Hey, you're that gymnast from the beach!" A woman stopped the trio by stone arches leading into an amphitheater. She wore an *I Love Lucy* T-shirt with black shorts and sandals.

"Yeah," Jordan replied hesitantly. She didn't recognize her or her friends.

"We're staying at the resort, too! You were so impressive! The sand didn't hurt your feet?" The red-haired woman threw out a dozen more questions, each more personal than the last, which Jordan answered quickly. She didn't want to be rude, but Sam and Liddy were several paces ahead.

"Have a great vacation," Jordan finished.

"You, too! Maybe we'll see you around."

She caught up with her friends as the lady kept walking the other direction.

"You normally like being the center of attention." Sam smirked.

"She wouldn't quit. I would've given her my first-born to just go away."

Sam scoffed. "You'd make an awesome mother, as soon as you're willing to make a commitment to a man."

Jordan stumbled. "What do you mean by that?"

"You so lovingly pointed out my faults in Santa Cruz, I think it's only fair we address yours."

Irritation crawled up her spine. "Okay, let me have it."

Sam stopped, and pulled off her sunglasses. "I love you, but you're a serial dater. You have the most stringent litmus test on men than anyone I've ever known. I think because you're afraid of failure."

Jordan's chest tightened, and her mind flustered. "Care to explain that?"

Sam's expression turned sympathetic. "You are the life of every party, and you are a blast to hang out with. But I don't think I've ever seen you have more than four dates with a guy. You split before it has a chance to get serious. You always give an excuse why he wasn't the *right* one. Tony was too short, Max was too clingy, Paul's job was too time consuming."

"There's nothing wrong with knowing what I want."

"That's just it, J. You won't settle for anything less than

absolute perfection. *No one* is perfect. *Everyone* has flaws, including you."

"I know that, and I'm not looking for absolute perfection."

"Yes, you are. Know how I'm sure?"

Jordan turned sideways. This wasn't going to be pretty, and her defenses started fortifying around her. "We better sit down for this." *Before I walk away.*

Jordan and Sam plopped down on the concrete bench just off the beach, but Liddy remained standing. Probably to keep her from running.

"You told me your father was extremely critical," Sam started. "That his love had to be earned. The only way you felt any affection from him was after winning a meet. First place only. Second wasn't good enough. You've brought that mentality into your love life."

"I love my father." Anger simmered in her stomach.

"I know you do. He's a wonderful man. Many of your best qualities come from him."

Jordan bit down on her tongue. "But?"

Sam pressed her lips together, obviously sensing Jordan's defiance. She pulled her sunglasses off to look in Jordan's eyes. "Let me give you an example. Would you think less of a man because he had cancer?"

"Of course not. I've never done that."

"I'm being hypothetical. You never would, I know that. But, say you start dating a man who hates dogs. I know you.

That would be a red flag and you'd probably drop him the second you learned that. But, if you stayed and heard him out, maybe he had a traumatic experience as a child where he was mauled by a dog. Would you judge him then?"

Jordan took a deep breath. She wanted to say no. Her friend described a legitimate fear, and she would never make fun of someone for that. But she really loved dogs, too.

"Your silence is telling me you would honestly give up the hypothetical perfect man if he was afraid of dogs." She put out her hands, as if weighing the two options. "You would love the dog more than him?"

"I hate *what if* games."

Liddy shook her head. "J, you constantly play *what if*. What if he lets me down? What if he plays me for a fool? What if I fail?"

Jordan pursed her lips, the tart margarita aftertaste turning bitter on her tongue. "This trip has gotten way too serious. We didn't come down here looking for the mythical perfect man. We came down here for a break and a fling. Can we get back to that, please?"

"Of course." They both stood, and Sam hooked an arm in Jordan's. Preventing her from walking off. "Jordan, we love you."

Jordan glared over the beach, refusing to meet her gaze. "I love you, too. Even when you're a pain in the ass."

"Comes with the package. Now, let's get back to the resort and get our drink on."

Chapter EIGHT

ZAC WATCHED SIMON very carefully during their shift. He'd blended a few frozen margaritas for the guests at the start of the dinner rush. Inside the main bar, the pair covered the restaurant's drinks, along with anyone passing through the main lobby. The back waiters didn't have a lot of time for talking or socializing tonight. The resort was packed.

"Did you hear about the party tomorrow?" Simon filled eight shot glasses with Patron. "Big ass pool party with *hors d'oeuvres* and fancy cocktails. They're gonna move the disco DJ out to the deck, cover the pool with those heavy-duty, clear plastic tiles."

"Like the New Year's bash?"

"Yep. Honeys will be out in mass." The blond bartender flashed him a toothy grin, a strand of hair falling over his brow.

Zac didn't answer. Ever since his chat with Detective Lacruz, he wasn't sure he could trust Simon. After all, the guest robberies hadn't started until around the time the new guy had been hired. Not to mention, the man was addicted to one-night stands with both guests and staff as well. Or so Zac had heard.

"You working tomorrow?" Simon asked. He twirled a few liquor bottles and poured more drinks, flashing his pearly whites for the pair of women in front of him.

"Late shift. You?"

"No. Think Marco would trade with me? I could really use the extra tips at the bar."

"Good luck with that. Marco has seniority, and management wants the most experience for the big parties."

"No harm in asking."

Zac kept a discreet eye on Simon's hands. If he were drugging customers, there were too many opportunities where Zac couldn't catch him, just by the way the bar was positioned.

But so far, everyone seemed to be enjoying themselves. He hadn't heard any reports of customers too drunk to walk, a possible sign of being drugged.

After a small lull in the rush of customers, a gasp came from the end of the bar. "Oh my gosh!" One of the earlier ladies searched around her barstool. "I can't find my purse!" The pair searched all around.

"Where did you last see it?" her friend asked.

"Someone turned in a lost purse a little while ago." Simon threw his dish towel over his shoulder, and set his arms on the bar top. "What does it look like?"

The woman described it.

Simon smiled. Then reached under the counter, and pulled out her purse.

"Thank God," she squealed.

"You left it in the waiting area."

He proceeded to flirt with the pair for the next ten minutes.

The line of drink orders piled in, and Zac had to fling a lemon wedge at Simon to get his attention back on work. Zac wouldn't be surprised if the guy ended up hooking up with both of those women later. *I'm taking more of the tips tonight, since I'm doing the heavy lifting.*

When there was finally another lag in the requests, Zac took a quick break out on the pool deck. He rang Miguel Lacruz.

"Zac, *mi amigo. Que pasa?*"

"You still looking for that suspect in the burglaries?"

"Do you have something for me?"

"Nothing concrete. Just, not rubbin' me the right way." He pulled a fresh towel from the stacks by the pool and wiped the sweat from his neck.

"Gut feeling kind of thing?"

"Yeah. Probably nothing, though." Zac tossed it in the laundry bin.

"Whatever you have, I'll take it."

DESPITE THE SUNBLOCK, heat radiated off Jordan's

body.

More lotion. She didn't have a sunburn, but after their fun-filled day, her skin had already absorbed a healthy dose of vitamin D. The ladies had returned from shopping and hung at the pool drinking frou-frou cocktails and playing a few rounds of water volleyball.

To Jordan's disappointment, Zac was stationed at the inside bar until closing. Liddy, however, was all too happy to be outside because Marco worked the pool bar.

Eventually, they returned to their room to get ready for formal night which consisted of a seven-course, five-star meal.

The *maître d'* sat them by the bay windows, with the stunning view of the sun dipping below the horizon over the water.

"To Liddy." Sam held up her glass of merlot. "May her rendezvous with Marco be as *all-inclusive* as Mexico should be."

Liddy giggled.

"Amen," Jordan replied. The trio clinked glasses.

Jordan wore the black dress she'd bought in Santa Cruz last year. The halter-style dress hugged her breasts perfectly, and prominently displayed her best feature, her shoulders.

Sam's strapless coral sundress accentuated her hourglass figure. In Jordan's opinion, Sam was the prettiest of the three. Up until last year she was also the most conservative. Then, their vacation had shown Sam just how much fun life could be. Now, with Chase's influence, she loved her body. She'd started wearing clothes that made her look like Helen of Troy, complete with blonde wavy hair.

"You should wear that on your honeymoon." Jordan winked at Sam.

"I think we may go skiing or take an Alaskan cruise, instead."

Liddy lit up like a Christmas tree. "How fun! I love winter vacays."

"Ugh," Jordan replied. "You're supposed to go somewhere hot and heavy on your honeymoon, so you can lounge around in your suite naked all the time. Not someplace cold."

"Says who?"

"Every single wedding magazine I've ever seen."

Sam smirked. "Since when do you read wedding magazines?"

"What woman hasn't? When you're a little girl, a teenager, or perhaps a bridesmaid in her best friend's wedding? Wink wink."

"Fair enough. But this week isn't about my wedding preparations. It's about Liddy. So, where are you and *Señor* Loverboy going tonight?"

Liddy's cheeks tinted pink, wearing the silly love-stricken smile they'd often seen over the years. "I think Polo has found her Marco."

Sam chuckled. "Houston, we have a winner."

"He seems very nice," Liddy offered by way of justification. "He wants to show me Old Vallarta, also called the Romantic Zone." She grinned from ear to ear.

Sam's eyebrows lifted. "Well, be careful."

"Good for you, babe. This trip *is* mostly for you."

Liddy hid a blush behind a bite of crab cake. "I'm meeting him by the fountain after dinner."

"The romantic zone." Sam grinned at Jordan. "Cocktails and dancing, or something more intimate?"

"Not sure. I wanted to have dinner with him, but he said he had a few things to do first. So, I'll be late tonight." Another blush.

"Good for you, girl." Jordan raised her glass to Liddy. "You deserve a fling."

"So do you. Zac seems really sweet."

Just hearing his name made her tummy flutter. "He's off at eleven and we're going for a drive."

"Maybe tomorrow you can rent a ski boat or something and enjoy Mother Nature all to yourselves." Liddy winked.

"Fantastic idea." Jordan swirled the wine in her glass. "Mexico really brings out the vixen in you. I'm so proud."

"Who knows, if tonight goes well enough, maybe I'll use the idea myself."

"You should. When he sees you in that mulberry sheath dress, he'll want to rip it off you."

"I hope so." Liddy giggled through another sip of wine.

Jordan couldn't help but smile. Their entire trip was

worth it for that gorgeous expression on her friend's face. Frank wasn't even an afterthought for Liddy anymore.

Hallelujah.

"Looks like you two have fun evenings planned." Sam leaned back in her chair, stretching her long neck. "I could almost be jealous."

"What are you going to do?" Jordan asked. "Please don't tell me hole yourself up in the room and work on your computer."

She smiled. "Sounds like me."

"Sounds like the *old* you."

"She could always try Skype sex with Chase." Liddy finished off the last sip of wine.

Jordan pointed at Liddy. "She gets fantastic ideas when she drinks. Let's order her another glass."

"Sorry. I need to leave if I'm going to meet Marco."

"I'm happy for you, girl," Sam replied.

Liddy stood, and gave each girl a hug over the back of their chairs.

"Be safe," Sam kissed her cheek. "Have fun."

Jordan sighed, really looking forward to her own rendezvous with Zac. "That's what these trips are for."

Chapter NINE

SEEING ZAC WAITING for her in the lobby made Jordan's tummy flip, like she was a ridiculous, impressionable teenager.

When he spotted her, his grin nearly turned her knees weak. He walked over and gave her a small peck on the cheek. "Hello, beautiful."

His sugary, scent with tinges of citrus made her mouth water. "Hello, handsome."

Jordan still wore her dress from dinner, but had changed into more casual sandals, and sported her new fedora. One of the things she loved about this dress was the ability to make it as fancy or informal as she needed with just a few accessories.

His gaze roved down her body, and back up. "You look exquisite. Formal night with the girls?"

She shrugged a shoulder. "We doll ourselves up every now and then, just for our own pleasure."

He grinned. "I appreciate that . . . *very* much. Nice hat."

She tipped the fedora ever so slightly. "Thanks. You free and clear?"

"Yup. Let's get out of here."

He opened the door to his Nissan Sentra, and she climbed inside.

Gentlemen do still exist.

The coziness in the small space and his subtle masculine scent filled her with a warm sensation she hadn't experienced with a man before. She curled into the seat beside him and stared at his profile. Strong, defined, with long lashes that made the butterflies in her stomach go crazy.

"So, where are we going?" she asked.

"I thought we'd drive along the coast."

"Sounds good to me."

He pulled the car onto the dark road, the streetlights overhead glowing. "So, tell me your story."

"My story?"

"What makes you tick? How are you still single? I can see you're good at gymnastics. Is that your sport of choice?"

"Uh-huh. I've been doing gymnastics since I was a kid. My parents put me in tumbling to get ready for peewee cheerleading, and the coaches told them I was a natural. And I liked it a lot more than cheerleading. Trained hard for years, and before I knew it I was competing for the US Olympic team."

He glanced her way. "No shit."

"No shit. But I missed it by two-tenths of a point. I'd

hurt my knee a few months before, and it cost me my chance."

"Crap. I bet that hurt like a bitch."

On so many levels. "I was disappointed, but not as much as my dad. I could've tried out again, but I decided to take advantage of a scholarship and go to college instead."

"Wait, a scholarship for gymnastics?"

"No, academics. I was valedictorian of my graduating class."

Zac's eyebrows lifted, and he was silent for several beats.

Maybe she'd sounded too boastful. Chatting with him was so comfortable, the words just flowed. She bit her lip.

"Wow," he finally said.

The quiet type. If that's all he has to say, then I must be coming off too strong.

"So, I graduated UC Berkeley, and took a job as a gymnastics coach at the local high school. Thought out trying to coach some of my athletes to make the Olympic team, too. I love it." She smiled just thinking about her vivacious students. "That's me."

"That's you." He nodded. Then turned the wheel around a deep bend up the hills. The farther up they went, the more stars sparkled in the sky through the high trees. "You said something about your dad. Is your mother still alive?"

That's a strange question. "Yeah. Why?"

"You mentioned your dad being disappointed. Was your mom, too?"

Zac didn't miss a thing. Funny, though. She hadn't been

that focused on her mother's feelings. "She was proud of me for even getting to that point. Sure, disappointed that I got so close and missed out, but my father more so. He . . . he's very driven. Ever since I first started gymnastics, he's pushed for the Olympics, and well, when I didn't get it . . ." Her words trailed off. How exactly could she explain her father without making him look like an asshole?

The silence in the car was uncomfortable to the point of her almost bailing on the date. She'd poured out a lot more information about herself than she expected, and he's silent? Jordan could practically hear the gears turning in his mind.

What is he thinking?

"Your turn. What's your story, Zac? I don't buy the spring break thing. Are you a permanent vacationer?"

The corner of his lip curved up. "What's that?"

"Someone who escapes from responsibilities to live in paradise."

His smile faded on that comment. "There are a few of those down here. But not me."

"So, tell me."

He sighed. "I grew up in upstate New York. My parents are busy professionals, commuting to Manhattan daily. My grandmother moved down here years ago with her second husband. When she got sick, I came down here to help her."

Her heart cracked a smidge. A grandson helping his sick grandmother. She nearly winced at how crass she'd sounded earlier. "Where's her husband?"

"He died some time back."

"And how's your grandmother now?" She held her breath, afraid of the answer.

"Doing better. She's in remission, but she's slowed down recently."

She kept her sigh of relief silent. "I'm glad she's doing better. Do you miss New York?"

"Sometimes. I miss my family, and I go back to see them when I can. But I love my grandmother, and the beach too much to move back."

They arrived at a raised plateau that overlooked the ocean. Zac pulled off the road to a small gravel lot. "C'mon."

They got out of the car and walked to a railing. The dark ocean spanned before them, a rippling carpet extending beyond the horizon. Moonbeams bounced off the waves as they came crashing ashore, like endless sparklers dancing across the surface.

"Wow." The breeze furled her dress up around her thighs.

Zac casually slipped his arm around her shoulders and pulled her closer. She nestled into his side, loving his warmth encapsulating her.

"Do you live with her?" Jordan referred to his grandmother.

"Yes. Nice little house on a hill where she can see the ocean. Early on, it was important that I be there."

"Of course." She wasn't sure if she should ask, but the

words just came out of her mouth before she could stop them. "Will you show me?"

He looked down at her, his look penetrating to her soul. "Okay."

ZAC REINED IN the flood of thoughts and emotions when being this close to Jordan. Alone with her.

When she spoke of almost making the Olympic team and being valedictorian, he instantly felt three-feet tall. He hated to admit it, but he hadn't accomplished much in his life. Or at least his successes paled in comparison as if he were a slacker or a freeloader—which had never bothered him before.

Jordan was an overachiever, no doubt about it.

And for some unknown reason, she wanted to spend time with him.

He took it for face-value. Whatever attraction sparked between them was temporary. She was on vacation, and he knew what that entailed.

At the end of the week, she'd check out. Of the resort, and his life.

Fair enough.

That didn't seem to matter whenever he thought about her, or watched her from across the pool deck. Especially didn't matter when he danced with her. Definitely not now as she sat next to him in that amazing dress with her legs crossed, the fabric revealing just enough of her thighs to make his mouth water. He was drawn to Jordan like a dog with a new bone.

The energy shifted in the car when she spoke about her father. He must have been the kind of man who expected only success from his children.

Zac often wondered about parents like that. As if they lived the life they never had through their children. Pushing their own dreams on them, whether the kid wanted to or not.

How much of that affected Jordan?

His parents barely had time for him growing up. That's why his grandma meant so much to him.

Instead of pursuing the topic any further, he'd dropped it. Maybe he'd ask her more about it later, but until then, as much as she wanted to reveal, he'd welcome it.

They pulled into the driveway to his grandmother's house, with all the lights out except for the front porch.

"At this hour, she's likely asleep."

"That's okay," she answered.

They quietly entered through the front door, and he led Jordan by the hand to the kitchen. "Can I get you something to drink?" he asked softly.

"Water is good, please."

He clicked on the light over the stove, and grabbed a bottled water and a beer from the fridge.

Jordan looked around the open room. Her skin shined in the soft glow of the kitchen light. So beautiful, like caramel or honey. Energy buzzed off her. The contagious kind that made him feel awake. Alive.

"Nice home." She smiled.

"It is. Makes her happy." That was really all that mattered. Zac didn't date much, and more importantly, had little reason to bring women to the house. His grandmother took priority in his life. He didn't know if he'd ever get married, but perhaps at thirty-one he didn't feel the rush.

"I see that." Jordan pointed with her chin to the rooster cookie jar and grinned.

He chuckled. "She's had that thing forever. Come'ere. Let me show you her pride and joy."

Zac laced his fingers between hers and led her out back. He flipped on a light and held the door open.

"Whoa," Jordan breathed out. "This is incredible."

Even in the dark with only the dim porch light, the tremendous garden was overwhelming. The lush greenery, flowers and towering bushes spread out to encompass most of the backyard—all layered and strategically planted to create an oasis of natural beauty. Vines with hundreds of little white flowers climbed the fence. Small, stone statues of praying cherubs and a flower-covered cross sat underneath a beautiful wooden arbor, covered with orchids. "On her good days, I can find her out here. She loves to garden."

"She's brilliant. Your grandmother has one hell of a talent."

If Zac thought Jordan was beautiful inside in the dim lighting, out here in grandmother's garden, she was perfection itself. Like Eve in the Garden of Eden. The breeze caught her dark locks, fluttering against her face...

He itched to run his hand through her hair, caress her cheek, breathe in her energy.

She smiled at him, and it nearly knocked him over. She took his hand and tugged him toward the cushioned wicker loveseat. "Let's sit."

"Okay." He forced himself to take a breath. "Let me turn off this light so it doesn't bother the neighbors."

Zac sat next to Jordan, his thigh flush against hers. He sighed, trying to relax even as her perfume sent his heart racing.

"This is certainly a romantic spot." She gestured at the flowers. "How fortunate for you when you bring women here."

He glanced her way, her big brown eyes so sure and confident. "I don't bring women here."

Her eyebrows lifted, and silence stretched between then.

"Well, I'd hate for all this to go to waste," she finally said with a soft smile on her face.

A shot of pent-up sexual energy shot straight to his dick, and his heart kicked in to double-time.

Chapter
TEN

ZAC'S GREEN EYES had never seemed so dark as right then. Jordan hoped she wasn't pushing him too far, but life wasn't any fun without risks. She wanted Zac, and there was only one way to find out if he wanted her, too.

She smoothly straddled his lap as her dress gathered up her thighs.

His warm hands cupped her waist. He grinned.

Wrapping her arms around his neck, she put her lips to his, letting a simple kiss grow into something hotter. "I like kissing you."

She kissed him again and he met her with equal passion. Tongues mingling, her center warmed with each passing moment. His erection pressed against her, and she rocked her hips gently into him.

He growled, and clasped the back of her neck, taking the kiss deeper. After several beats, he pulled back and stared straight into her eyes. "You're an enigma, Jordan. I don't think I've met anyone like you before," he whispered.

"Is that a good thing?"

"A very good thing." He claimed her mouth again.

God, she could kiss him all night. She wanted more. To taste him. Would he let her?

She broke the kiss. "Zac," she panted, "let me have a little more. Let me taste you."

His gaze locked on hers, as if half-stunned by her request, and half-eager to let her do as she pleased.

She slid her body to the ground before him, the grass cool against her legs. Kneeling between his thighs, she stroked him over his pants.

His head fell back. "Jordan." The plea was weak.

"Please." She reached for the button and grasped the zipper on his shorts.

He gripped her shoulders, perhaps to pull her away, and yet he didn't.

She gently eased down the zipper, and reached to fist his cock. To set him free.

He was beautiful. Long, thick, and damn hot.

She brushed a thumb over the tip, and his eyes briefly fluttered closed.

She lowered to take him, slowly licking his length, savoring his masculine taste.

"Oh shit." He pulled off her hat and wove his hands through her hair, fingering her locks.

She didn't stop. She couldn't. She loved it too much.

He sank lower in his seat, giving her more of him.

"Mm," she murmured over him. Taking in all she could and sucking on the way back up.

His moan spurred her on. She fisted him, working him harder and faster. She loved pleasuring a man, and for Zac it was all the better.

The grip on her hair tightened, but she didn't let up, drinking him in and sucking him dry.

"Fuck," he growled through his climax. His body went limp.

She carefully put him back together, and rose. He grabbed her hips and pulled her onto his lap, wrapping his arms around her and pulling her close.

"You're incredible," he breathed in her ear.

She smiled and held him while his breath recovered, his face pressed against her chest. "I'm glad you enjoyed it."

Pushing against her shoulders, his eyes narrowed. "Enjoyed it? I loved it." His head tipped. "Now, I think it's your turn."

She chuckled. "Oh yeah. Where do you want me?"

He looked at her with his beautiful, heated eyes. "Up on your knees, sexy."

She swallowed, and rose to her knees, lifting her weight off his lap. Anticipation energized her whole body.

Lifting the hem of her dress, his warm hands grazed over her hips, her tummy, and her mons. He slipped his fingers under her black lace thong, continuing his caresses.

She clasped the hem of her dress. She didn't know how

much longer she could wait. Everything pulsed, ached, screamed for release. Would she have to beg?

Thankfully, he didn't leave her waiting long. He hooked his fingertips under her thong and dragged it down, stretching the lace over her thighs.

His jaw dropped. "Sweet Jesus."

"What?" Her heart skipped a beat.

His hand covered her sex, and stroked back and forth gingerly. "Jordan, you're beautiful. I love that you keep your hair."

Was he serious? "The way I'm built, I don't have much choice."

He glanced up at her and smiled. "You make that sound like a bad thing." A single finger slid through her center and back again. "I love this. The more the better."

Is he fucking serious?

"Ah."

He stroked her again and she lost conscience thought. Under his expert touch, the world turned to a delicious haze. Her head fell back, and he continued his ministrations—soothing, stroking, sliding.

"You are so fucking beautiful." His voice rough with lust, he dove a finger into her channel.

Jordan almost lost it. This could be the most erotic thing she'd ever done. She wanted to be naked—no damn clothes in the way—and bask in skin against skin, but she didn't want to stop him. His hands were pure talent.

He added another finger and stroked her mercilessly . . . slowly. Finally, his thumb circled over her clit.

The tingles from the beginnings of her climax fought its way to the surface.

With his free hand, he gripped her hip, as if he feared she'd fall. He might have been right as he dove into her harder, pulling back and pushing in faster.

The sensation ratcheted up and sent her spiraling down. The rush of energy coursed through her body, and the need to scream her release powerful. She had to cover her mouth to hold it in, and whimpered and bucked in his grasp.

When it was over, she collapsed in his lap, panting, gulping in air.

His hand slid away, and he held her as she calmed, kissing the top of her head.

Without doing any of the work herself, he slid up her panties and adjusted the skirt of her dress back into place.

"*That* was incredible," she parroted his words. Maybe one of the best orgasms she'd ever had.

He smiled. He kissed her long and slow one last time. "Let's get you back."

"Will I see you tomorrow?"

"Do you scuba?"

Her heart sighed. "I love scuba."

"Perfect. Meet me in the hotel lobby at ten in the morning." She felt his grin against her neck.

Jordan nodded. She would've smiled if she could feel

her face. The next day couldn't come soon enough.

HOW IN THE world do you have the energy for this?" Sam breathed in the rich scent of her coffee from room service.

"How do you not? We're in paradise!" Jordan finished her stretches, and adjusted her sports bikini.

"You were out so late last night, and the sun is barely up this morning. Isn't there a rule about time between sleep and scuba?"

Jordan laughed. "That's flying in an airplane. And it depends on how deep you go, or something. I have to be downstairs in fifteen minutes to complete the resort's scuba course, or I can't go out on the boat with them today."

Still in her pajamas, Liddy pulled her hair up into a loose ponytail and sat beside Sam on the bed. "Let me get this straight. Zac's a bartender, a home health aide to his grandmother, *and* a scuba instructor?"

"Not an instructor. He loves to scuba, and is helping out the dive master today." Jordan slipped on her tank top and flip-flops, and grabbed her exercise shorts. "How did things go with Marco?"

Liddy hid a blush behind a sip of coffee.

"Oh, now you have to tell us." Sam swiveled on the edge of the bed to give Liddy her full attention.

"Let's just say the man has *expert* fingers."

Sam started laughing, and Liddy's blush deepened—to the point where she actually had to fan herself.

Jordan bit her bottom lip, hoping they wouldn't notice her own blush. Because however good Marco was, Zac could probably give the man a run for his money.

"We didn't go *all* the way," Liddy finished, curling her leg under her as she sat next to Sam. "But there's nothing wrong with heavy petting. Not on vacation."

"You've got that right, sister." Sam wrapped her arm around Liddy and squeezed. "You've got that glow."

"The one *you* had in Santa Cruz," Jordan added, stepping into her shorts.

"What about you?" Liddy asked. "Was Zac the perfect gentleman for your coastal drive?"

"Took me up to the point to see the ocean view, and then to his grandmother's house to see her garden. Talk about tropical oasis."

"Uh-huh," Sam nodded, and circled her hand like she was pulling a rope for more information. "And then what?"

Jordan put on her fedora, adjusting it a little too long in the mirror.

"Come on. What happened?" Liddy pressed.

"I'll just say Zac could win that heavy petting contest."

Liddy chuckled.

Sam snickered. "Both my girls have struck gold on this trip. What did I tell you?"

"*You* struck gold," Jordan corrected. "We're still panning in the creek bed, finding some gold dust. And it's damn fun, that's for sure."

"That's what you're going to wear for scuba diving today?" Liddy asked. "A fedora?'

"Wanna come with me?"

Liddy shook her head vehemently. Sam scrunched up her face.

"Seriously?" Jordan. "You're breathing underwater, how cool is that? It's the closest thing to being in the womb. You just float along as the ocean hugs you in warmth."

Sam held up her finger. "First of all, no. That's not hugging, that's a rip current. And you'll never be seen again. Second, the closest thing to being in the womb is the Seven Sacred Pools in Hawaii, where there's no undertow to drown you."

"I think you're just scared."

"Snorkeling is my limit." Sam stood, and grabbed a piece of paper from the desk. "Write out your will before you go. Can I have your shoe collection?"

Jordan held up her finger, copying her superstitious friend. "First, no, never. Second, you're as adorable as you are annoying on a power trip. I'm not going to enable you by writing out anything. I'll see you all for dinner."

"I think she's just doing this to spend more time with Zac," Liddy smirked. "You'll probably just stay on the boat the whole time, mackin' and disturbing the fish."

Sam chuckled. "Cuz the mask and flippers combo is so darn sexy."

Jordan flashed a fake smile. It wasn't so much the mask and flipper combo, it was the hot, wet, chiseled abs she looked forward to. "What are you two going to do?"

"Tan by the pool, and drink. My two best moves." Sam winked.

"You have far better moves than that," Jordan replied. "Those are just your favorites. Other than Chase's moves." She waggled her eyebrows, and then headed for the door.

"J," Liddy called. "Be careful. If you get hurt, I'll kick your ass."

Jordan held open the door, and smiled. "I will. See you tonight."

"Have fun."

SOMETHING ABOUT ZAC standing on a boat gripping the railing as he smiled at Jordan said this man was comfortable in his own skin. He exuded a quiet confidence and certain kind of humility.

She strolled down the dock, holding her rented mask

and flippers under her arm.

He held out his hand to help her aboard. The rest of the guests joining them might as well have never existed with his concentrated stare.

She took his hand, and pulled herself into his frame.

He kissed her cheek, light and airy. Careful not to wrap his arm around her. After all, he was working. Then he whispered in her ear. "You look glorious this morning. Like you had a *really* good sleep."

"With yummy dreams."

He winked.

She stepped down and put her stuff with the rest of the gear.

As everyone took a seat, Joaquin, the Divemaster, spoke to the group, reviewing the rules and what everyone could expect. The trip out to the first dive spot took nearly an hour. Jordan spent the time enjoying the strong breeze and soaking up the tropical sun.

And watching Zac assist the captain. He was on shift, so she didn't want to distract him or get him in trouble. She loved how he handled the boat like it was second nature. He knew he had her as an audience, and yet he did nothing with flourish or boast, which Jordan found vastly appealing. For the life of her, she couldn't say why. She had always been attracted to alpha males. Zac was far from her typical love-interest, but in some respects *exactly* what she needed.

When they reached the dive spot, he threw the anchor

overboard and stood on deck with bare feet.

The choppy waters had most others stumbling and gripping the railing, but not Zac. Like a ninja, he kept his balance as if he knew the rhythm of the ocean in his soul.

A trio of high school girls ogled him as if he were a Hemsworth brother, or Poseidon himself.

Yeah, Jordan could relate. She knew that fascination well.

At least as an adult, she could keep her infatuation under control.

Mostly.

One by one, the guests jumped into the waves, water cameras and selfie sticks in hand.

Jordan sat on the bench, and slipped on her BCD vest, securing it to her chest. She double-checked the airflow in the regulator.

Zac pulled his shirt over his head to don his scuba gear, giving Jordan the first glimpse of his bare chest.

Damn. Poseidon, indeed.

She was thankful she was still sitting, because that man could knock her over faster than any wave.

He strapped the BCD vest to his chest, and grabbed his flippers and mask. Then held out his hand. "You ready to go, buddy?"

"Every day of the week, and twice tonight."

He grinned, a slight blush gracing his cheeks that had nothing to do with the sunshine.

They jumped off and went under together.

The second the water closed overhead, the world silenced. The only thing she could hear was the slow intake of air through her regulator, and her own heartbeat. Bubbles danced to the surface on exhale, and she watched them climb to the obscured sunlight above.

On the way down, she plugged her nose and equalized the pressure through her ears, repeating the same motion every ten feet. The water cooled the farther down they went. At the bottom, the sand was a light gray spotted with gnarled coral, blending in with the rocks.

Zac rapped on his tank a few times to get her attention.

Even with the mouthpiece, she noticed his smile because his eyes narrowed slightly through the mask. The water couldn't mute those jade irises.

Her breath caught. Amplified by the sound of the air tank.

Zac motioned forward toward the rest of the group. He let her swim ahead, him keeping back at an arm's length. He'd probably done this dive a hundred times. His job was not just to be her buddy, but keep the group together on the tail end. Make sure no one got lost. She thought there was nothing like the feel of the water enveloping her like a blanket, weightless and freeing.

She was wrong. Zac's presence behind her on this adventure of freedom amped up her excitement.

Light glinted off the abundant fish in a flash of silver,

but they skittered away when she came near. A few yards ahead, a moray eel peeked out from a hole in the rocks.

Zac slipped his fingers in hers, and squeezed. He pointed to the other side.

A large manta ray glided along the seabed, the wingspan as large as a loveseat. The white spots on its dark back reminded Jordan of her mom's Australian Shepherd, Brandy.

They floated along, keeping up with the group at a short distance. The guests veered around a bend in the rocks.

Zac's hand slid up the back of her knee along her thigh.

She turned her head, and let her feet drop, so she floated vertically.

His hands skimmed across her hips, smooth and cool. Then he removed his mask.

Her breathing escalated. *What the heck is he doing?*

He blinked against the water, and took one last breath on his regulator. Then pulled it out, letting it float beside him. He motioned for her to do the same.

She took another breath, and pulled it out.

He tugged her toward him. He wrapped his ankle around her calf, and cradled her neck in his hands.

His lips touched hers, soft and gentle. Then he brushed his tongue against her seam, and she opened for him.

His hot mouth melded with hers, countering the cool water against her cheeks.

Nothing was as hot as the heat pooling between her thighs.

The salty sea mixed with his own taste, and she wanted more.

Jordan deepened the kiss, as much as she could with her mask still in place. But Zac pulled back.

He put the regulator back in his mouth, and took a deep breath.

She did the same. Her pace was faster like he'd taken her remaining air with that kiss. Bubbles came out of his unit faster, too.

She grinned against the mouthpiece. She'd taken his breath away, as well.

Chapter TWELVE

ZAC COULD BARELY catch his breath.

He'd been dying to kiss her ever since she set foot on the boat. The first one wasn't nearly enough.

Jordan's hair floated around her head. Even in a BCD vest, the woman looked irresistible. She wore a sport bikini like she was born with it.

She fanned her face.

He laughed and nodded, bubbles dancing to the surface.

She'd lit his libido on fire with just her lips.

After he replaced his mask and cleared out the water, he let his eyes readjust before taking her hand to catch up with the group. They'd just about completed the loop, and the ship's anchor line was in sight.

He still tasted her in his mouth, against his regulator. Sweet and minty, mixed with the salt of the sea.

Good thing the water was cool and could help tame his hard-on just in time for the group to ascend.

Everyone climbed on board, and removed their gear. He

had a lot of prep work to get ready for the second dive site, which they'd reach in another thirty minutes. But all he wanted to do was plaster himself on Jordan. He loved the way she made him lose control.

Her skin practically glowed from the sunlight bouncing off her wet body. Sun-kissed face, tan and toned frame, and a physique to die for. In her two-piece, anyone could tell the woman was a gymnast from her sculpted arms, buff thighs, and those abs.

After cleaning up and making sure the guests were taken care of, he climbed topside to check in with the captain.

He leaned over the railing to spot Jordan below.

She'd reclined on the bench, letting the sun and air dry her off before the next dive. She held her fedora on her head, to keep the wind from tearing it off.

He'd already tasted her once before, a brief dalliance with her vixen side in his grandmother's garden. Seeing her like this, on display in close quarters . . . a taste wasn't nearly enough.

She looked up at him, and her smile widened.

He smiled back. *Damn, I'm putty.*

They slowed to the next site. He climbed below, threw the anchor over, and relayed instructions for the dive. The dive master sent him a look that told him he knew exactly what was going on. And Zac needed to watch it.

He made sure to behave himself for the second trip below.

Once again, he swam behind Jordan, letting her enjoy the scenery. He'd been to this site countless times, so his fascination was watching her experience this world for the first time. He loved the marvel on her face.

The dive went by fast, and before long they climbed back aboard the boat to head in. The waves had grown choppier while they were under, and the wind had kicked up.

The ride back to the resort was longer, and he tried to finish his duties quickly, but the group of high school girls kept interrupting him. Trying to flirt in their juvenile way.

It was cute, and he turned them down easy, not wanting to hurt their feelings.

Jordan chuckled a few times and let him fend for himself.

The captain turned on the overhead speakers, and filled their ride back with Spanish pop music. The teens started dancing until they realized the boat rocked a little too much, which forced them to sit.

Zac sat next to Jordan on the fiberglass bench, a half a foot away from her body, but still enough distance so he wouldn't get in trouble with the boss. Damn, how he wanted to pull her into his lap. They watched the shore come slowly back into view. The air thickened in the late afternoon, with a few clouds rolling in. Sunset was a few hours away.

"You get to do this a lot, don't you?" she asked.

"Get hit on by high schoolers, or scuba?"

"Both."

"Mmmhmm."

"I can see the attraction."

He looked sideways at her.

"The scuba, I mean."

"Ouch."

She laughed, and caressed his shoulder—which granted them a few glares from the girls across the boat, but he didn't care.

"You know you're hot shit, don't deny it."

"Just doing my job," he replied.

"And loving every second of it."

"No, I love the water. And meeting people like you."

"People like me?" she asked.

"You know you're hot shit, don't deny it."

"Fine, I won't. Thank you." She laughed again.

He loved the sound, so full of energy and life.

"But seriously," she continued. "Is that a requirement to work at a resort down here? Ridiculously good looking, moonlighting as models?"

He chuckled. "I moonlight as a grandson. Nothing glamorous in that."

"Time well spent. I wonder if Marco has the same kind of generosity."

He tilted his head. "Why do you ask?"

"Liddy's become quite attached to him."

"Hey, she found her fling."

"Looks like it."

"He's a fun guy."

"I saw him the other day at the Malecon."

Zac frowned. "Really? What was he doing?"

She shrugged. "Stopped some kid's soccer ball from bouncing in the street. He was too far away for me to talk to him."

"That's a tourist spot."

"Yeah. A popular one. Why?"

"Most locals steer clear of it. Too many tourists."

"Is he a good guy? For Liddy?"

"He's a blast. Known him almost a year." Zac leaned back, letting his arm rest discreetly against her back. "The resort is having a pool party tonight, with extra food and drinks. Complete with fire jugglers. Going all out with the fancy stuff. Should be fun, if you're interested."

"Yummy. Something special going on?"

He shrugged. "Probably to help boost morale, settle guests' fears from the burglaries."

"The what?"

Zac bit his tongue. He'd forgotten he wasn't supposed to say anything, per management's instructions. But the words came out before he'd realized it.

"People have been robbed?" she pressed.

He dropped his voice and leaned closer. "I shouldn't have said anything. A guest was robbed Wednesday night. She got very drunk, and it may have happened while people were distracted trying to help her."

"Oh, crap."

"The detective thinks it might be a resort employee."

Her eyes widened.

A knot tightened in Zac's stomach just thinking about that. Someone he knew, worked side-by-side with, could be targeting women. Right now they were just robberies, which was bad enough. But what if the crimes escalated to something worse? Zac had a burning desire to keep Jordan close. He'd always considered himself a passive man, and never engaged in aggressive behavior, but when it came to Jordan, he'd kill the guy who lay a hand on her.

"So, are you working tonight?"

"Yes."

"Good, because I'm going to stay close by you."

He grinned. *Just what I had in mind.* "Good idea."

The twinkle in her eye changed to something more serious. "When are you off?"

"I close. Off at three-thirty or four."

"Come to my room after your shift."

He held his breath. He should say no, but damn. Just looking at her, her big brown eyes pleading with him, knowing the passion that lay beneath . . . How could he tell her no? "It'll be late."

"I'll be up."

He bit the inside of his cheek. "What about your girlfriends?"

"They won't mind. Besides, they'll be asleep in the other

room."

"Okay."

The corners of her perfect, pink mouth curled. "Okay."

Chapter THIRTEEN

DANCING ON WATER while the bass music thumped through the air filled Jordan with an electric charge buzzing through her body. The clear flooring placed over the pool just for the party was a brilliant stroke on the resort's part.

They'd probably underestimated the sheer number of guests showing up. Ten times as many people danced around the edges of the pool than in the disco inside. Either the resort had a huge influx of guests the last twenty-four hours, or people invited friends from off-resort.

Sam and Liddy pumped their hands in the air to the rhythm, and light danced off the sequins on Jordan's tank top. The other end of the pool was open, with people bouncing beach balls around. One landed on Liddy's head. She laughed, and hit it back.

A waiter passed by with a tray of tube shots, neon colored vials full of tequila, vodka, or rum. A few people grabbed some.

"I need a drink," Sam shouted over the music and went

to grab a shot.

Jordan called her back. "Let's get something from the bar, instead. You never know what are in those."

Sam nodded. The three girls snaked their way through the crowd to the pool bar.

Jordan winked at Zac as they walked up. Another line of people waited for drinks, but Zac had three bottled waters waiting for them.

"Helps to have connections," Liddy laughed. She guzzled the ice water.

Jordan's skin glistened with sweat. The humidity spiked this evening, but that hadn't slowed anyone down.

"That floor is so awesome," Sam said to Zac as she leaned against the bar. "Hopefully it can hold all that weight."

"It can." Zac grinned. "Been thoroughly tested by all the employees."

Marco strolled over from the other side of the bar, and reached across the counter for Liddy's hand. He fluttered kisses along her knuckles. "Are you having fun, *chiquita*?"

"I'd be having more if you were out there with me."

His suave smile widened. "Later, *te prometo*."

"What's that?" Liddy asked.

"I promise," he replied with a wink.

"What can I get for you ladies?" Zac asked. He cast a quick glance at Jordan, the knowing look to remind her she'd promised that he would make all their drinks tonight. Just to be safe.

She hadn't told the girls about the robberies. There was no sense in scaring Liddy, whose overly dramatic reactions to those kinds of things would've killed the mood for the night. Besides, with Zac looking out for them, she wasn't worried.

"Lava flows, all around." Sam sucked on an orange slice from the garnish tray.

"You got it." Zac slapped the counter and pulled three glasses from the freezer chest.

"Wait a minute," one of the Canadian guys called from the other side. "I was here first. All I want are three beers."

"Hold on a sec, ladies." Zac went over to the guy and helped him out.

The two bartenders and their backwaits flew around the bar like someone hit the fast-forward button on a drink-pouring ballet. Their moves were seamless and coordinated, each performing their duties with precision and ease. One would blend, the other would shake a tumbler, then move into garnishing while simultaneously pouring shots, each step merging with the next, having the other's back.

Jordan couldn't keep her stare off Zac. A few women around the bar tried to flirt with him, and he'd always respond with a smile or a chuckle never took it too far. As if appearing available, but never *being* available.

Because the man was definitely *not* available. At least not this week. He was all Jordan's.

He whirled back around and finished their lava flows.

Marco topped off their drinks with umbrella straws and

pineapple garnishes. He threw a cherry into Liddy's, and winked.

Jordan caressed Zac's hand.

He leaned in and muttered into her ear from over the counter, "You look incredible in those shorts."

She tugged at the hem of the black fabric, stretching just past her ass cheeks, which made her short legs look longer, especially in her high heel wedges. She pulled him closer. "They are easy to remove in a hurry."

Zac groaned and bit his lower lip. His lustful stare was so enticing.

She couldn't wait for after the party.

The girls held up their drinks.

"As my grandfather would say," Jordan began, "*Arriba, abajo, al centro, y adentro! Salud!*"

Sam smirked. "What does that mean?"

"Glasses up, glasses down, to the front, and gulp it down."

They laughed, and clinked their drinks and downed them in a few guzzles.

Loud drums boomed over the space, and fire lit up the stage on the far end.

Two bare-chested men twirled flaming sticks into the air, drawing the crowd closer. Whistles pierced the air when they tossed the fire batons back and forth at each other, while spewing flames from their mouths.

Jordan glanced at Zac a few times, his face flickering in

the light cast by the flames. The heat escalated higher, her skin glistening more with every fire toss.

The show only lasted a few minutes, ending with a Lady Gaga remix thumping through air.

Liddy squealed. "Dance floor! Now!"

Jordan blew a kiss at Zac, and followed the girls.

ZAC HAD WATCHED the trio of women as close as he could the first hour. How could he not, with Jordan's legs all shiny and lasting for days? The silvery crop top shirt and *short* shorts gave him an instant hard-on. With granite abs like hers, it was the perfect look to show off her stunning figure.

What he liked most was how casually she turned away the guys who hit on her. With how packed tonight was, there'd been quite a few already. Every few minutes, she'd lock eyes with him from across the patio, and smile. Or wink. Or blow him a kiss, and he'd growl inwardly.

End of shift couldn't come soon enough.

But he had to stay focused. He and Marco and their backwaits were in their rhythm, and supervising everything took extra effort.

A backwait called in his ear for more tube shots. The chefs had created the specialty drink earlier today, and kept them in the chiller for the party. But he'd warned Jordan to steer clear of those because he hadn't prepared them himself.

He wasn't sure who to trust. He found himself keeping an extra close watch on Simon. If the newest bartender were responsible for the drugging, he wanted to catch the man in the act.

More orders flooded in, and Zac struggled to keep up.

A few minutes later, he heard a shout, followed by a scuffle on the dance floor.

He looked over.

Jordan hobbled off with Liddy's arm draped over her shoulder. Sam trailed behind.

The girl swayed and her heel slipped on a plastic tube shot, threatening to tip her into the pool.

Sam and Jordan pulled Liddy back, and struggled to get her into a lounge chair.

The blonde grinned and laughed, muttering something. Her arms flailed, and her face looked drowsy.

"That chick is wasted," someone laughed from the side.

Sam bolted for the bar. "Water," she called at Zac.

He grabbed a bottle and handed it over. "What's going on?"

"Something's wrong with Liddy." She didn't explain more, and went back to the girls.

They tried to get her to drink some, but Liddy laid back on the chair instead. She started singing Lady Gaga, the words coming out in a slurred mess.

Jordan looked over at him. Their gazes locked, and hers read fear.

Zac didn't hesitate. He jumped over the counter and charged over. "What's wrong?"

"She's not making any sense," Jordan replied trying to keep her voice down, but over the music it was hard to hear. "She's only had the two drinks. We know what she's like when she's drunk, and this is *not* it."

"Did she have any of the tube shots?"

Sam shook her head. "Just the lava flow and a beer."

Jordan knelt in front of Liddy and tapped her cheek, trying to get more water into her.

Just the lava flow.

A frigid razor sliced down Zac's back. Like someone had unzipped his spine. He looked up at the bar. Only the backwaits, trying to help the flood of guests.

Marco was gone.

"I'll be right back." He rushed to the bar, and dialed for hotel security and an ambulance. Guests called for drinks, some angry with how long they'd had to wait, but he ignored them. "Better get management down here, too," he finished on the phone.

Marco was still missing.

He hurried back to the girls. "Security and the medical staff are on their way. Make sure she gets more water."

"Where are you going?" Jordan asked, her eyes full of concern.

"Don't let her out of your sight."

Chapter FOURTEEN

ZAC RACED DOWN the hallway into the elevators, and punched the button for Jordan's floor. Technically, he was abandoning his post at the bar. A fireable offense, but this was more important.

The elevator took far too long to reach the sixth floor.

"That son of a bitch," he whispered under his breath, trying to keep his rage in check. "All this time. Be wrong, Zac. Please, *be wrong*."

The second the doors opened, he bolted around the corner.

Jordan's room was at the end of the hall. The window in the alcove outside their door overlooked the pool, the multi-colored lights bouncing off the top of the palm trees.

He didn't have to walk that far.

Their door opened, and out came Marco.

Carrying a backpack, the zipper nearly bursting.

The man took a few hesitant steps toward him. "What are you doing up here?" his friend asked.

"I should ask what you're doing in Jordan's room," his voice shook with rage. "But that's obvious."

Marco kept walking toward him, casually. "It's a long story, *amigo*. I've never hurt anyone, *lo juro*."

"Don't you swear anything to me."

The closer the man came, the less Zac recognized him. The strange look on his face, the shifty steps, a completely different gait as he moved down the corridor.

"The cherry. Was it always in the garnish? Or did you stick it down the straw?"

He shook his head. "I have a lot of debt to pay off. My mother, with her health, and—"

"That's bullshit. You're gambling again."

Faint beads of sweat shown on Marco's forehead. "I'll cut you in on it. For half. Just let me walk by."

Zac tightened his fists. "Drop the bag."

Marco sighed, and lifted his chin.

"Why didn't you just come to me if you needed help? Instead of this shit."

He raised his chin higher. "*Lo siento, amigo*. But a man takes care of himself." He swung a punch so fast, Zac couldn't react. Other than to let it collide with his jaw.

The shot ricocheted through his head, and a blinding pain ripped at his chin.

Marco dashed by, but Zac spun and hooked his arm around the guy's neck, then yanked back with all his strength.

Marco landed on his back, the thud echoing down the

hall.

Zac yanked the bag off his arm.

The strap ripped. The zipper busted open, and the girls' things fell out. Wallets, passports, jewelry, and more.

The Mexican spat some vicious curse words, and he kicked Zac in the leg, followed by a strong jab to the gut.

Air whooshed from his lungs, and his stomach threatened to heave.

Marco scooped up the bag and the passports, and regained his balance to bolt down the hallway.

Adrenaline raced through Zac's veins. With a sharp pull on his former friend's shoulder, he threw the hardest punch he had, connecting with Marco's temple.

The man grunted. Dropped to the floor like a sack of sand.

Zac's knuckles howled in agony, just as the throbbing registered in his jaw. He needed to call security, and Detective Lacruz. But first, he slid down the wall and waited for the carpet to stop swirling.

He stared at the lump of a jackass that used to be his friend—still unconscious with Jordan's passport in his hand.

The idea of this guy drugging all those women...

What if he'd done worse to others they didn't even know about?

What if his intentions were to rape these women?

To assault Liddy?

What if he originally had targeted Jordan?

Zac's stomach pitched. The thought literally made him sick.

From down the hallway, the elevator dinged. A second later, two security guards turned the corner and spotted him on the floor.

He held up a hand, not yet ready to speak.

"Zac," one of the guards, Pedro, called out to him. "Are you all right?"

He nodded. "It was Marco."

"Is there anyone else in there?" Pedro felt for Marco's pulse, then secured his hands behind his back with zip ties. "*Pinche cabron.*"

"Don't think so."

The other guard went into the room.

"How is Liddy?" he asked, and slowly stood. He staggered to stay upright, rubbing the pain in his jaw.

"EMT's are with her now. You should take it easy. That's a nasty shiner on your chin."

"I'm all right." He flexed his hand, which screamed in protest.

"Have the ambulance check you out."

"Clear," the second guard called from the room. He came out with his hands on his utility belt. "That place is ransacked. Zac, the hero of the hour."

Not comfortable with the title he joked, "Catching thieves wasn't part of the job description."

"Then it's time to ask for a raise."

Zac shook his head. "This bastard was my friend. He's been doing this for God knows how long and I missed it. Pretty sure I won't be getting a raise."

Pedro stood in front of him. "Everyone missed it. But *you're* the one who stopped him. Now, go down to that woman, and be the knight in shining armor. Because not many men get to be *that* guy."

"Absolutely right, *guey*," the other guard added. He slapped Zac on the shoulder.

The knight in shining armor. He rubbed his jaw. *Hurts like hell.*

Chapter
FIFTEEN

LIDDY SLEPT COMFORTABLY in her bed, her breathing deep and even. The paramedics had helped her quickly, and the resort doctor had put her on an IV for a few hours. He assured Sam and Jordan she would be fine. She hadn't needed a trip to the hospital, which was a huge relief.

Their clothes and belongings had been scattered throughout the room, except for the items that Marco had stolen. The police had returned their things, and now Sam wandered throughout the rooms resetting things to right.

Jordan sat next to Liddy, checking her pulse and breathing every so often. Probably just being overly protective, but she couldn't help it.

Out the window, the pool party still thundered on, but it was far less crowded. Cops and paramedics showing up to a report of a drugged woman tended to thin out the ladies, which then thinned out the male crowd as well.

They'd seen Marco escorted out in handcuffs by police as they brought Liddy up to the room. He had a huge knot on the side of his head, and was clearly disoriented.

Jordan rubbed the arch of her foot, her muscles aching from her dancing shoes. "This is all my fault."

Sam huffed, and shoved some clothes back in the drawer. "Don't you dare," she whispered, and pointed to the door.

Jordan rolled her eyes, and climbed off the bed. They went into the other room, so they wouldn't disturb Liddy. Though with the drug and alcohol mixture, she wouldn't wake for several hours.

"I'm the one who pushed so hard for her to hook up on this vacation," Jordan seethed. "When she found Marco, I encouraged it."

"We all did. The guy's a con artist. The police told us he'd been playing this scam for months. And guess what? That bastard won't be doing it again anytime soon. Because of Zac."

Because of Zac.

Jordan ran her fingernails across her scalp. She still hadn't seen him since he'd charged off. At the time she hadn't had a clue where he was going, but the security guards had told her everything afterward.

Zac had figured out it was Marco—then single-handedly charged into the fray, confronted the thief, and body-slammed him. Followed by knocking him out cold.

She'd wanted to run up to Zac and throw her arms around his neck, thank him a thousand different ways, but the police had kept him for questioning.

He wasn't responding to texts, either.

Sam sat on the couch, rifling through their passports one more time. "Should we go home early tomorrow? Cut the trip short a day? This kinda sucks all the wind from our sails."

Jordan curled up beside her, tucking her feet under her. Her first instinct was yes, get the hell outta Dodge. Her friends' safety was her main priority. But her heart cracked at the thought of never seeing Zac again.

"We'll let Liddy decide in the morning. Whatever she wants to do." Jordan sighed.

"You know her," Sam replied. "Her trust issues are legendary, even before this. Now..."

Jordan nodded, and pinched the bridge of her nose. "Did you call Chase?"

"Yeah. He's livid, but knows we're all okay. Have you talked to your parents, yet?"

Jordan shook her head. "I won't wake them up for this. If we decide to leave early, I'll call my dad and give him the new flight time." She bit her tongue. "I can just hear him now. 'Shame on you for not being more careful. If you don't protect your friends, no one will watch your back.'"

"In the next breath," Sam countered, "he'll tell you to depend on no one except yourself. No-win situation, there. But my personal favorite ... Remember the one thing he always told you?"

Jordan reluctantly looked at her friend. "What?"

"If you fall off..."

She humphed. "Get your ass up."

Chapter SIXTEEN

A LIGHT RAP came at the door. Jordan's breath shook.

She strode to the door, looking through the peephole to find Zac standing back with his hands in his pockets. She opened the door and smiled. She'd been waiting all day for him. To be alone with him.

He wore the collared knit resort shirt that showed off his strong shoulders and chest. The same one from earlier. She held back a frown when his smile didn't reach his eyes.

"Hi."

"Hi. Come on in."

He hesitated briefly and walked through the door.

She inhaled and caught his masculine scent, a scent she'd quickly associated with Zac.

"Would you like a water?"

"Yes, please."

She retrieved two bottled waters from the mini-fridge and handed him one, then noticed the dark shadow on his jawline.

She winced. "Even heroes get bruises. Did you ice that?"

He nodded. "It doesn't hurt that much."

"How about we go out to the balcony?" She motioned toward the closed bedroom door. "Sam and Liddy are sleeping."

"Okay." He pushed open the sliding door, and waited for her to pass. "How is Liddy?"

She sat on the outdoor sofa, pulling her legs onto the cushion. "She's fine. No risk of seizures at this point, especially after all the IV fluids. The doctor said she'll be better tomorrow."

He took a seat next to her.

"What did they all say to you? The cops? The hotel?"

"Well," he took a deep breath. "I still have a job."

She snorted. "I should hope so. You cracked their case."

"Yeah, but I should've seen a lot earlier. Or Marco was just that good at hiding it." He shook his head.

"Management has comped our stay, as well as offered us another week's stay for free. Probably hoping we won't sue."

"That's the least they could do. You should take them up on it."

She rested a hand on his.

He flinched, and yanked it back. His knuckles were bruised, and a few cuts marred the skin.

"I'm sorry. Let me get an ice-pack for you."

"I'm okay." He grabbed her hand with his good one.

She met his gaze. Her heart pounded so hard she could

barely breathe. "Thank you so much for what you did." She shook her head and glanced down. "Never in a million years did I think something like this could happen to us. I am so grateful for you."

The corners of his lips rose slightly. "You're welcome. I'm sorry Marco even made it this far."

"You had no control over that."

He nodded, but broke eye contact. He kept his troubled stare on the floor.

The knot in Jordan's stomach grew. *Did Zac not want to be here?*

"Zac, is everything okay?"

He paused, and his eyebrows pulled together. "I shouldn't be here."

"Why?" The knot in her stomach turned to lead.

Now, he finally looked at her again. "You . . . I like you Jordan, and . . ."

"Do you want to be somewhere else? With someone else?"

"No. God, no. It's just . . . after everything tonight . . . This is a booty call."

She exhaled, and gave him an understanding smile. "It's alright, Zac. I want you here."

He stared out into night and the dark ocean, as if warring with his thoughts. "I'm not this guy. I don't do one-night stands, never take advantage. I was raised better than that."

"Zac, please look at me." She softly stroked back a hair at his temple. "I like you a lot, and I'm really glad you came up. I've been thinking about this all day. Please, stay."

"Jordan, I can't stop thinking about you." His voice was barely above a whisper.

His concern for her, his respect for her, only made her madder for him.

God, where has this man been hiding?

She cradled a hand at the back of his neck and leaned forward to claim his firm lips. He parted for her, his tongue meeting hers with equal passion.

She mewled.

His arms wrapped around her body, pulling her into his torso. He kissed her like there was nothing else in the world he'd rather do. "The thought of anything happening to you, drove me insane."

His warm hands stroked her back and the top of her ass. His every touch built the tension in her low belly. She wanted him, to feel him, all of him. She tugged at his shirt, lifting.

He stood and pulled the shirt over his head, dropping it to the floor.

God, he was beautiful, standing so perfectly close to her. Her hands caressed his firm, toned chest muscles, and ran along his etched ab muscles. His physique was strong, but not bulky. She could stare at him all day like a fine sculpture.

He grasped her upper arms, raising her to her knees on the sofa. Holding the hem of her tank top, he lifted off her shirt, dropping it onto his.

With tentative hands, he slid his hands up her arms and over her breasts, smoothing a thumb over her taut nipples.

She moaned at the sensation.

"You are perfect," he whispered against her lips as he pulled her close, her naked chest flush with his.

His warmth flooded her, his kiss, his hands on her ass, pushing her against his hard length. He overwhelmed every inch of her.

She gripped his shoulders, wanting more. She wanted to crawl up his body, touching everywhere possible, his skin searing hers.

"Jordan," he breathed through their kisses.

She reached for his khaki shorts, unfastening the button and zipper. Quickly, her hands enveloped him, eliciting a throaty groan.

"I want you, Zac. I want to feel all of you."

She looked up into his dark eyes and knew he felt the same way. All hesitation had vanished.

He toed off his sandals, then pulled a condom package from his pocket and pushed his shorts and briefs to the floor.

She gasped.

He didn't waste a moment when he was reaching for her boy shorts, pushing them over her hips. She laid flat on her back as he pulled the shorts away, adding them to the pile.

When his entire body covered hers, she thought she'd gone to heaven.

She cupped his cheeks to capture his mouth in a hungry kiss. She hooked her legs around his ass, feeling his delicious erection press against her core.

"Zac," she begged.

"I know." He broke the kiss and trailed kisses down her neck to her breasts.

Her back bowed off the sofa when he sucked her hardened nipple into his mouth, his tongue toying with it. He repeated the glorious torture to the other breast, leaving her whimpering for sweet release.

His tongue dipped into her navel, and his kisses continued south. With a fingertip, he slid through her wet core while his lips traveled down one thigh, licking and sucking.

A single trickle oozed down her crease to her ass. He smoothed her center more, barely touching her clit.

God, she was going to go insane.

She spread her legs farther apart, and gripped the armrest overhead. Her hips lifted slightly, pulsing to gain more pressure from Zac's touch. It was useless.

He continued his oh-so-gentle caressing over her swollen lips, while kissing, nipping, licking her inner thighs at the same time.

She was on the verge of spiraling out of control, when his tongue finally plunged into her core and swiped firmly up and around her clit.

"Oh, God."

He did it over and over, pressing against her engorged clit.

Her climax broke in a fury of lust, rocketing through her body. She muffled a scream in her arms, as Zac's tongue relentlessly swirled.

Before she could push him away from the extreme sensitivity at her sex, he dove two fingers into her dripping channel, stroking her while he laved her clit more. Pushing, twisting, making her delirious with pleasure.

"Zac," she cried out again as another orgasm pummeled her, not letting her catch her breath.

Finally, the climax subsided, leaving her boneless. She panted, her eyes closed to everything.

"Watching you climax is like a wet dream," he whispered over her lips.

She swung her arms around him and kissed him deeply, tasting herself in his mouth.

His cock poised at the crux of her inner thigh. At some point he'd sheathed himself.

She reached for him and brought him to her entrance.

With a deep growl into her neck, he pushed inside her. "Jordan, I won't last long, but we won't be done."

"Okay." She wouldn't fault him. He had taken care of her like no other man had. She couldn't always come, but something about this man—it was like he'd known her body for years. He knew just how to touch her, how to play her like a piano.

She wrapped herself around him, holding him close, as they moved together. He felt glorious inside her, creating a connection sweeter than heaven. Some foreign emotion swelled inside her. One she couldn't define, but she never wanted it to end. This to end. *What the hell am I going to do when Monday comes?*

Chapter
SEVENTEEN

ZAC HELD JORDAN'S naked body tight against his. Somehow it wasn't close enough. He wanted closer.

The connection he had to her scared him to death. How could he feel so strong about someone he'd only just met? She'd leave in a few days, if not earlier, after everything that had happened.

He shoved the thoughts from his mind. He would enjoy the time they had together until she left, and pray he didn't regret one second.

She had touched him in a way no other woman had.

They snoozed for several minutes after making love on the balcony sofa. When he awoke, he was instantly hard for her.

"Mm. This is a nice way to wake up," Jordan whispered in a sleepy voice.

He kissed the hollow of her throat. "I agree." His hands roamed her body as he had full access to her front. Her head arched back when his hands toyed with her pointed nipples, and moaned. He slid one hand down her flat stomach to her core and gently massaged her tender lips. Wetness spread to his fingers.

Christ, he loved making her feel good.

She lifted a leg, her foot resting on the back of the sofa while he dove a finger into her channel.

"God, Zac. How do you do that?" she panted. "How do you know just what turns me on?"

He continued his movements, slow and gentle and deliberate, until her moans turned into pleas.

He rose and yanked a condom from his shorts on the floor, and covered himself in record time.

He climbed back over the woman that would likely occupy his dreams for the rest of his life. "Baby, put your legs on my shoulders. Easy as mounting the balance beam."

She grinned, and did as he asked.

His dick slid inside her. He whispered out a curse. She felt like paradise.

He lowered his torso, watching her face for any sign of discomfort and kissed her lips. "Are you okay?"

"Yes. Perfect. Don't stop."

"How am I supposed to say goodbye to you, Jordan?" It was a question he didn't want to know the answer to, and didn't wait to hear. He covered her mouth with his, savoring every taste and nuance. Memorizing it for later.

He slowly pumped into her until he couldn't take it anymore, on the verge of exploding himself. But he would never leave her wanting. He pulled out, and holding onto the backs of her thighs he leaned down and laved at her tender pearl, pressing and twirling until she screamed out his name.

He raised up and dove into her, feeling the remains of her orgasm clutching his dick. His mouth swallowed her moans. He was out of his mind for her—pumping, driving deep, wanting to feel all of her he could. His orgasm ricocheted throughout this body. The strongest one yet. When his body finally drained, he collapsed over her, panting in her ear.

"That was amazing," she whispered.

He gently pulled out and sidled next to her, his arms wrapped around her. "When do you leave? Spend the day with me."

Her smile lit up her drowsy eyes. "I'd love to." Then quickly faded. "But, it's up to Liddy if we stay. If she wants to go home tomorrow instead of Monday, I can't say no."

Zac bit the inside of his cheek. "I get it. I don't blame her. But . . . "

"But if she chooses to stay," Jordan cupped his face. "I'd love to see you."

"I'll pick you up at one for lunch. Give you a few hours to sleep."

She nodded. They rose and gathered their clothes, catching a few glimmering beams of sunlight waking the world to a new day.

He kissed her one last time at the door, exhausted and

oddly invigorated at the same time. "Sweets dreams."

MAYBE NATURE IS sending me a sign," Liddy proclaimed in a seemingly foul mood. Dramatic and a bit overbearing, yet understandably so. Very Liddy.

What a relief!

Sam and Jordan looked at each other. "How so?"

"Guys. What if Mother Nature is saying, 'No damn guys for you.' I mean, I like a cute guy and he turns out to be a thief *and* a liar."

Sam bit on her lip, and Jordan grinned. "I don't think that's what Mother Nature is trying to tell you."

"But the important question is," Sam reached across the bed and covered Liddy's hand with her own, "should we check out today and go home?"

Liddy's eyes rounded. "Why? I have no man waiting for me there," Liddy motioned with her arm pointing north.

Jordan glanced Sam's way. "Okay, our girl is back to her ol' self."

Thank God, because Jordan's stomach still turned when

she thought about not seeing Zac that day.

"What I need is comfort food. Let's order breakfast."

Neither girl dared to tell her it was noon. Sam called room service, and as they waited, Jordan decided to bring up the subject of Zac.

"So, Liddy, I'm not sure how to ask this." Jordan looked up from the dresser drawer she rifled through. "Zac has the day off and wanted to hang together today. How do you feel about that?"

She held her breath. Fully expecting the answer to be unsure and uncomfortable.

"I don't mind. He's really nice, J. I like him. Go be with him." Liddy glanced at Sam. "Sam and I have one last day to work on our tans. We can do more shopping, and eat lunch in town. I need to get a snow globe for my collection."

"Are you sure?"

Both her friends nodded without reservation. "Just no more alcohol for me. Nothing but bottled water today."

She smiled, incredibly relieved to see Liddy feeling so optimistic, considering the circumstances. The unconditional love from her friends was so humbling at times. She wrapped her sweet friend in a hug.

Liddy hugged back. "Go enjoy yourself."

Her trip to the lobby was bittersweet. She got to see Zac one last time. It would be brief, but she'd take it.

JORDAN INHALED AS she sat on the wooden bench

outside the resort, waiting for Zac. The sun shined bright and the sky was so incredibly blue, they couldn't have asked for a better day, their last day, to spend together.

After only a few minutes, Zac pulled up in his signature Nissan Sentra, and she smiled. How it suited him—simple styling *and* practical.

He stepped out of his car, and circled the back to pull her into his frame. "Good afternoon, beautiful." He smiled back.

"Afternoon." She rose on her toes to kiss him, tilting her head to keep her fedora in place.

His arms instantly enveloped her.

She loved the feeling of his warmth around her, loved his smell, and without question, his kisses.

"How's Liddy?" he asked. Concern tinged the edge of his eyes.

"Much better than I expected," Jordan replied. "The doctor did a great job. She woke up in fairly good spirits."

"That is such a relief." He opened the door for her, and Jordan settled in. When he rounded the car to get in, she continued. "They're going shopping today."

"What a coincidence. So are we." They each buckled in.

"We are? Where?"

"That's a surprise. First, I thought we'd eat lunch outside." Zac motioned with his chin to the backseat where a tote and cooler rested.

"I love picnics."

They drove with the windows down along the coastline for several minutes before Zac pulled off the highway onto a dirt road, heading up the hill. The area seemed more remote, only a few *haciendas* visible, with most of the terrain tall trees and bushes. Blooming flowers scented the thick, humid air. Jordan trusted her tour guide. Especially after everything they'd been through. As long as she could spend the day with him—however few hours they had left—she'd go anywhere.

Zac steered the car to the side of the road, lined by lush green palm trees. "C'mon."

He grabbed the food from the car, and she followed him through the trees to a little clearing. She gasped.

If the view from her hotel balcony was lovely, this was nothing short of spectacular. The ocean glittered as far as the eye could see, the coastline cutting into the blue sea in uneven points and currents with a few thin sandbars parallel to the shore. The resorts poised along the inlets and cove gave the seemingly untouched landscape a luxurious, European feel. The sight was worthy of a *National Geographic* cover.

"This is incredible."

He grinned.

"How did you find this?"

He shrugged a shoulder as he set up a picnic area. "I like to adventure. It was a complete accident, but I never forgot how to get here."

She couldn't take her eyes off the beauty before her. The breeze wasn't too strong, and helped lower the humidity.

"Well, sir, you sure know how to impress a girl."

She stretched her legs out on the quilt beside him, draping her feet over his shins, and tore into the fare he brought—sliced meats, cheese, fruit, fresh tortillas, and bottled water.

"It's not much," he started, as he caressed her knee. "But I figure it will hold us until dinner."

"It's perfect." She leaned forward and stole a quick kiss.

They sat in peaceful quiet, Jordan absorbing the atmosphere and the feel of him beside her.

"Let's play 'This or That'." Jordan sat up at her idea.

He tipped his head. "Is this a truth or dare kinda thing?"

"You say which you prefer, like chocolate or vanilla?"

"Chocolate," he said with a grin. "Okay. I'm game."

"Me, too. I eat something with chocolate in it every day. Okay, next, ice cream or sherbet?"

"What the heck is sherbet?"

She laughed at his scrunched expression. "It's less creamy than ice cream, and usually fruit-based."

"Then I'm going ice cream on that one."

"Jeep or convertible?"

"Depends. Jeep during the day, and convertible at night."

"You can't have two answers."

"Of course I can. What's your answer?" His eyebrows lifted.

"Convertible, because I can go faster."

He grinned. "Then that's my answer, too."

She nodded, proud of herself for getting him to agree. "Coffee or coke?"

"No tea?"

Jordan smirked. "You don't strike me as a tea guy."

"You're right. Coffee. The darker the better."

"Ditto. Danish or donut?"

"Both. Especially with said coffee."

She giggled. "Bruce Lee or Chuck Norris?"

"No contest. Chuck Norris."

"Really?" she chuckled.

"A single glare from Chuck can defeat entire armies."

"I'll take your word on that. Snow skiing or water skiing?"

He glanced her way with a *seriously?* expression.

"Don't give me that look. You have to say it."

"Water skiing. Definitely." His voice rose an octave.

"Well, there may be a problem. I'm a snow skier. Black diamond all the way, baby."

"Too damn dangerous. Jumping out of a plane has fewer injuries."

"Who wants to jump out of a plane? One and done. Skiing can last all day, all week," she dragged out the last words.

"Okay. Have fun on the slopes," he said unconvinced. "Let me ask one. On the kitchen table, or on a boat?"

Jordan paused, her smile widening. "That's a tough

choice. You'd really do it on a boat?"

"I'm just asking about where you prefer to eat meals. What are you talking about?"

She punched him in the arm. Not hard, but enough to rock him to the side.

He laughed.

"Next, Angelina Jolie or Eva Mendes?" she asked.

"Neither! Jordan Beck."

"Ah. Good answer, *señor*." She placed her hand under his jaw and brought his mouth to hers. She kissed him sweetly for a beat, then stroked the tip of her tongue along his lower lip.

He opened to her for a slow insinuation of their tongues. He tasted like blueberries this time.

It amazed her how Zac could so easily mirror just what she wanted or needed.

As the kiss continued, she wanted more. She lifted her leg to straddle him, his growing hardness pressing into her. A faint wetness gathered at the apex of her thighs.

He broke the kiss, resting his forehead to hers. "We should stop."

"We should?" she whispered.

He cupped her neck, and smoothed a thumb along her cheek. "I've made special plans for us."

That sent a little fizzle through her. "What plans?"

He put more space between them. "How do you feel about having dinner at my house tonight? With my grandmother."

She didn't stop her grin. He actually wanted her to meet his grandmother. "I'd love it."

"First, the shopping surprise I promised. Then after dinner, I have more plans, too."

"Oh, a woman could get used to so many surprises. You should pace yourself."

"I'm going to make this day last as long as I can."

She planted a big, loud kiss on his lips, hungry for something else other than food. "You read my mind."

Chapter NINETEEN

GLASS PIECES SPARKLED through the storefront window of the specialty shop in Yelapa, enticing them inside. The store reminded Zac of an art gallery or a museum where the only medium the artists used were blown glass. Shelves and niches were filled with large and small shapes like fish, faces, bowls, and vases. Every piece unique and intriguing.

Jordan's eyes rounded to saucers. "Wow," she breathed.

"This place is really cool," Zac said. So worth the thirty-minute drive.

"How the heck do they make these?" She picked up a multi-colored statue of blue and aqua curling in a semi-circle to look like an ocean wave.

"No clue."

They slowly meandered the shop, taking in each item, the pieces gleaming in the sunlight. Jordan occasionally let out an *ooh* and *ah*, but they mostly walked in silence.

After a few short moments, an elderly woman approached, smiling. "*Hola*. Welcome. How are you both today?" Her English was excellent even though her dark complexion and accent revealed she was native.

"Hi. Do you know how they make these?"

"In the back of the store, we have a window where you can view the artists at work in the studio. Every piece requires a different glassblowing technique. And some things," she pointed up the wall to a decorative piece made with overlapping glass plates, "require spinning or rolling."

"Cool." Zac admired a plate made to look like a basket weave, the separate pieces intertwined flawlessly.

"If you want to follow me, we can watch them. I believe today, they are working on glassware sets."

They followed the sales rep to the back of the store and stood before a large window alongside other spectators to watch two men working. A large open-fire furnace, metal rods, tools, and several glass pieces sat on tables. One man held a plastic hose in his mouth as he blew into a reddish-orange glass ball, slowly increasing the size. The second artist pulled a larger vase-like shape out of the fire. Gripping the metal rod it was attached to, he swung it back and forth.

The shop lady pointed to him. "Stephano is elongating the piece while he swings it, before the glass cools. The average temperature of the furnace is about two-thousand degrees Fahrenheit."

"Dang! That's crazy." Jordan looked at him, her eyes twinkling in awe.

"During the week, we have classes open to the public

when the artists help people make an ornament for their tree. Will you be able to come back to participate?"

"No. What a shame. I leave tomorrow."

The woman's gracious manner never faltered. "Well, we're glad you're here now. Let me know if you have more questions."

"Thanks." Zac glanced at Jordan. "Do you want to keep looking around?"

"Yes, I'd like to find something for the girls."

He wrapped his hand around hers, and strolled through the rest of the store. "What do you think they'd like?"

There was so much to see that Jordan seemed oddly indecisive. She'd occasionally ask out loud *Would Sam like this?* Or *Would Liddy like this?*

Utterly adorable.

Finally, she discovered clear, round pendants with a different colored flower inside. Almost like the flower floated in a bubble. Jordan lifted one for closer inspection.

"These are so pretty."

"They are," he agreed. "It looks like each petal had to be made individually, then fitted together."

Her gaze locked with his, her eyes bright. "I think this is it." She nodded to the flowers. "I'll get one for each of us."

"Great idea."

"Liddy loves purple. This sunset orange for Sam, and of course, blue for me." She grinned.

"Ya' know? I think I'll buy one for my grandmother,

too." He pulled a red one from the display, and rolled it between his fingers. "You think she'll like this one?"

"All women like flowers." The smile on her face, the sheer joy, made Zac's heart skip a few times. He could stare at that smile the rest of his life.

The thought alone made his heart almost stop. *Not now, Zac. Focus on here and now.*

They wandered the store for several more minutes because there was so much to look at when Jordan let out a little gasp.

"What is it?"

"Look at this." She smoothed her hand over the crest of a blue and clear foaming wave. It had to be twelve inches tall.

"That's impressive. I can't imagine the work that went into making it."

"This would look so good in my sunroom." She lifted it slightly off the shelf, careful with its weight. "But there is no way I could bring it home. Too big and heavy."

She shrugged her shoulder, but the sparkle in her eyes faded.

"You sure?"

"Yeah. I have the pendants anyway."

They proceeded to the checkout and put them in little jewelry boxes.

On their return to his car, she stopped him, wrapping her arms around his neck. He loved how she had to rise up on her toes to kiss him. "Thanks for bringing me here, Zac.

This is awesome. The whole day has been awesome. I'll never forget it."

A rush of emotion hit his core. Making her happy meant the world to him. "You're welcome." Then he planted a little kiss on her lips, smiling through it.

As he drove to his *abuelita's*, Zac held Jordan's hand. The road traversed back up the hills and around several bends, then finally his grandmother's *hacienda,* nestled among trees at the top of the hill.

More than once he glanced at the clock, counting down the hours he had left with her. He scolded himself. He couldn't think about what wouldn't be. That was wasted energy.

Chapter
TWENTY

GRAM?" ZAC CALLED when he opened the door.

The second Jordan stepped in, the mouth-watering scent of pork and masa hit her senses.

"Those are tamales!" Jordan grinned. Her stomach jumped for joy.

A woman came around the corner wiping her hands on a towel with a red rooster on it. Her white hair was pulled back into a curly ponytail at the base of her neck. She took one look at Jordan, and smiled.

Zac's smile. The very same.

"Aren't you a doll?" Her face lit up like the Fourth of July. She moved slowly across the room with a slight limp.

Jordan met her halfway, so she wouldn't have to walk as far. The woman's hand was soft and wrinkly. "Very nice to meet you. I'm Jordan Beck."

"The San Francisco gymnast. Enchanting. I'm his *abuelita,* Eva Consuela."

"You're making tamales. I haven't had those in ages."

"I felt inspired. It's been a good day."

Zac kissed her on the cheek. "I can see that."

"Can I help?" Jordan asked. "I used to help my mother all the time as a kid."

"You're a sweetheart, my dear. They're already in the double boiler. But I was about to start making tortillas for enchiladas, if you don't mind."

"That was my job," Zac chimed in.

Abuelita patted his cheek. "And I love you for it. Please, go water my jasmine out back, *por favor*. Jordan and I have to talk about you behind your back."

"Some would consider that rude." He kissed her on the cheek again.

"When a grandmother does it, it's endearing."

He chuckled, and gave Jordan a wink before going to the garden.

"In here, dear." Eva slowly moved into the kitchen.

Jordan followed her, to where the masa scent intensified.

"It's clear where Zac gets his charm. And his smile." Jordan washed her hands.

Eva started rolling out the dough, and placed a chunk in the *comal*. "The charm isn't from me. That's all his father."

"What are they like, his parents?"

Eva gave a short laugh. "Driven. Exceptionally motivated, and singularly focused. I suppose you have to be if you live in Manhattan."

"What do they do there?"

"His father is in banking, his mother is a paralegal for the city. Commercial contracts or something."

"Wow."

Eva scoffed. "Needless to say, very busy. One would think their son would've grown up to be just like them." She smiled. "But not my Zac. So, what about you? What do your parents do?"

"My mother is a teacher, high school European History. My father is a retired Army colonel. Spends his days as the HOA president when he's not hovering over me."

She chuckled. "Fathers and their little girls. And you? Zac told me you're a gymnast."

"Coach. For the local high school. I tutor the ESL kids to maintain my teaching status, too."

"ESL?"

Jordan pulled down on the *comal,* pressing the dough flat. "English as a second language."

"Bilingual?"

"*Si, señora. Un pequeño.*"

Eva held her heart. "Manners, too." She patted her hand. "I approve."

Jordan chuckled. "For what, exactly?"

"To date my Zac."

She blushed, and smiled. "How many women that he's brought here have you approved?"

Eva tilted her head and gave her a funny look. "He hasn't

brought other women here."

Jordan blinked. "Seriously?"

Eva gave her a sad smile. "Poor guy hasn't had much fun since he moved down here five years ago."

Jordan raised her eyebrows. "Works at an all-inclusive resort and scubas whenever he wants. Sounds like a blast to me."

Eva turned off the press, and sat in the kitchen chair. The wood creaked as she slowly adjusted her body. The relief on her face was palpable. She glanced out the window at Zac, watering not only the jasmine, but the rest of the rose bushes as well.

"He may work there, and enjoys his shifts, but it hasn't been a pleasure cruise. Taking care of me, managing all my bills. I've had some health problems."

Jordan sat across from her. "I'm sorry to hear that."

The woman sighed. "When Zac was six years old, he was diagnosed with leukemia."

Jordan gripped her shirt over her heart. The thought of a little child suffering that way . . . no words. "He never said anything about that."

"Of course not. It wasn't a very pleasant time of his life."

Jordan swallowed hard. "May I have some water?"

"Yes, please." Eva stood to get it for her, but Jordan touched her knee.

"I'll get it. You sit and relax." She stood and found a glass in the cupboard. "Tell me more about him."

"His parents had to keep working to afford his medical bills. So, I moved in with them to take care of him. Lived with them while I took him to his appointments and treatments. Chemo, radiation, on that tiny boy's body . . . " She shook her head, teary-eyed. "In those two years, we became very close. Many rough days, and even harder nights. But my Zac pulled through. Such a fighter."

Jordan smiled, and set two glasses of water on the table. "He was very lucky to have a grandmother like you."

"Bless you, child. We do what we can for those we love. You'll see, when you have children."

Jordan blushed.

"Zac did so well in school. Smart enough for any college he wanted. His parents hoped he'd go to medical school. Help other sick kids." She frowned. "But I knew that wasn't for him. He'd had enough of doctors and hospitals."

"What did he want to do?"

"At first, he wanted to be a magician."

Jordan chuckled. "Really?"

"That was his favorite thing during those weeks at the hospital, when the magician would come and entertain. The kid spent so much time practicing with a deck of cards." She laughed. "But after high school, he went to a small college in New York, got a degree in communications, and took a job as a swim instructor. He didn't want to end up like his parents, working all the time."

"They didn't have much time for him?"

"Which is why enjoying his work is so important. Life is just too short."

"Yes, it is," Zac answered, the back screen door clicking shut behind him. "And you still have a lot of it left ahead of you."

Eva chuckled.

He kissed her on the cheek and then washed his hands. "Just smelling those tamales . . . I'm starving."

"Good things come to those who wait." His grandmother stood, and checked on the boiler.

Zac leaned back against the counter, crossed his arms, and stared at Jordan. "You have this adorable smile on your face."

"Funny, I was thinking the same thing about you."

"Easy, kiddos." Eva brought the rice and beans to the table. "Don't start drooling over each other yet. You'll contaminate the food."

An authentic Mexican dinner with Zac and his grandmother topped the glass shop. Jordan couldn't remember the last time she had homemade tamales. Or the last time she felt this at ease with a boyfriend's family.

Conversation flowed naturally, and Eva had just as quick a sense of humor as her grandson. When the plates were empty, Jordan offered to do the dishes.

Eva sat back in her chair. "Normally, I would never consider letting a guest clean up after me, but I'm beat." Even the skin on her face seemed to droop as she said the words.

"You get some rest, *abuelita*." Zac stood and kissed her forehead. "You've had an exciting day."

She smiled at him, then grabbed his hand, where his knuckles were still bruised. Her smile vanished. "I could say the same thing about you from last night."

Zac frowned. "I promise, it's not that bad."

"Miguel Lacruz called me. Told me what a help you were."

"A help? Must be another word for reckless and stupid."

"Be careful though. Your body doesn't heal as quickly."

"My body heals just fine. Thanks to you." He kissed her forehead again.

"Thanks to God for that."

He helped her from her chair.

"Thank you so much for this wonderful meal." Jordan gave her a kiss on each cheek.

The woman wrapped her tiny arms around her in a hug. "I hope to see you again, dear girl. Perhaps when I have more energy, we can go on a boat ride."

"I would love to."

Zac followed Eva to her bedroom, while Jordan cleared the table. Then she filled the basin and began scrubbing the plates.

Looking out the window over the sink, Jordan marveled at the garden archway, where she and Zac had fondled each other the other night. The heat rose on her face remembering those phenomenal hands. The flowers and bench looked different in the daylight. Brighter, fuller, more homey. A private tropical paradise right here. No wonder Eva stayed in Mexico all these years.

Soft hands glided up her waist from behind, then wrapped around her middle. Zac kissed her neck, and nuzzled her shoulder.

Jordan hummed her approval.

"Did you get enough to eat?" he asked.

"I could always use dessert," she murmured back.

She felt his smile against her skin. "That's for later. But I couldn't resist showing my appreciation." He fluttered more kisses along her neck.

She turned her head, and met his lips, melding their mouths as his hands moved up her stomach and cupped her breasts. Massaging lightly.

Her body instantly reacted. Aching to be quenched. "You better take it easy. I'd hate for your grandmother to lose her high opinion of me when I take advantage of you here on this floor."

Zac's soft laugh reverberated across her skin. "Fair enough."

"What did she mean by your body doesn't heal as quickly?"

He grabbed a clean dish from the counter and started drying it with a towel. "I was sick a lot as a kid."

"Leukemia," Jordan filled in the answer for him.

Zac shook his head. "Thanks, *abuela*," he muttered.

"Do you still have some side effects, from all the chemo?"

He put the dish in the cupboard, and took her hand. "I'm all good now."

Jordan's heart cracked a tiny bit thinking about a poor boy battling such a beast. It must have felt so lonely, so scary. What if he hadn't survived?

Although these days flew by, they were the best Jordan could remember in a long time . . . a very long time. She felt like herself. Somehow more free, and yet more grounded. She owed most of it to Zac. Because like her friends, his attention and affection wasn't conditional.

He spoke just what she'd been thinking. "Let's finish this and get out of here." The corners of his lips curled upward.

Chapter
TWENTY ONE

THE TREE FROGS chirped in the palm trees as Jordan walked down the lit path, letting Zac lead the way through the resort. The waves from the shore in the distance mixed with their song.

As they closed in on a bank of elevators, he asked, "Do you need to go to the room? Check on the girls?"

She lifted her phone, flashing him a text. "Nope. They're good. They're actually in the lounge watching *A Few Good Men*."

"Ah, yes. Movie night."

They followed the signs to the *Zafiro* wing.

"Where exactly are we going?"

He pulled a room key from his pocket, one with a picture of a sapphire etched on the back. "I have a friend in housekeeping. We get the executive suite until daylight," he said with a wink.

Her mouth instantly watered. She gripped his hand as he maneuvered through the hallway to the elevators, slipping in the key to gain access to the top floor.

When the doors closed, she grabbed his waist and pulled him into her.

Jordan claimed his mouth, urgent and needy.

He pressed his body into hers, his length already hard in his shorts.

She'd been dreaming of this moment ever since he left her early that morning. Since she stood in his grandmother's kitchen.

The doors opened far too soon, and she stepped out into the top floor suite entryway. The robin's egg blue marble floors extended into the living area with plush cream carpeting. But it was the floor-to-ceiling glass windows that stole her breath. The endless ocean set the backdrop to a romantically lit patio balcony. The suite was complete with sofas, a personal bar, and hot tub.

"It pays to have connections," Jordan marveled.

"It pays to be nice to everyone," Zac answered. "As long as we clean up after ourselves."

Jordan moved into the living room that led to the patio. Open double doors off to the side revealed the bedroom, with a romantic canopy bed set up for a couple, or perhaps a honeymoon. As much as that room called to her, she couldn't resist the hot tub.

The door slid open when Zac pushed a button on the wall. The jets started up with another button.

"Did you bring a suit?" he joked.

She flashed him a hungry smile. She scooped her hand through the water—the hot temperature perfect. "Who needs one?" She slowly began a little striptease.

His grin slowly melted into a ravenous stare as she peeled away her clothing, leaving her completely nude.

She closed the gap between them in three steps. "Mr. Durant, I do believe you're wearing too many clothes to properly enjoy the executive suite hot tub."

He grabbed her hips, crashing them hard into his torso. "You're sexy as hell."

Then his firm, demanding lips claimed hers before she could protest. Not that she would. Naked or not, being in Zac's arms was the only thing that mattered. More than sticking the perfect landing. More than the gold.

He plumbed her depths, sucking and licking with urgency.

She gripped his shoulders, clutching him as if he were the center beam, the sole axis keeping her in the air while life rotated around her.

Finally, he broke the kiss and pulled off his T-shirt, throwing it over his head. He made fast work of his shorts and shoes until he stood before her . . . gloriously nude.

And extremely thick, at full attention.

"C'mon." He stepped up and over into the hot tub, and offered her a hand.

She took the two steps up and followed him down into the steaming water, so relaxing it nearly hurt. "Oh, God it feels so good."

"That's just for starters." He pulled her into him effortlessly as she bobbed in the water.

She straddled him, flesh against flesh.

His mouth fastened to hers.

Jordan savored his taste and the way his hands caressed her sides down to her ass. Then he cupped her cheeks, pulling her flush over his eager cock.

She moaned through the kiss.

"I shouldn't want you so bad," he breathed over her lips. His thumbs glossed over hardened nipples before he twisted them between his fingers.

Her eyes closed, and her head dropped back. A loud groan built low in her throat, too much to hold back. Her long hair swirled in the water, soaking wet.

His lips nipped at her neck, but he never wavered from tormenting her peaked nubs.

She flexed her hips, gently riding him, desperate to alleviate the need.

Zac continued, and her achiness grew. Water sloshed against the sides, and spilled over the edges.

"Oh, God, Zac," she said through her ragged breath.

His tongue trailed down the front of her neck. "Baby, don't stop."

"Mm." She rode him harder, and if it were possible, he grew thicker with her grinding. She stroked her clit against him, the ridges of his silky cock making her delirious.

Her climax built until she could no longer hold it in. In her haze, she was vaguely aware of his orgasm too, his cock pulsing against her sex.

She brought her head to rest on his shoulder, letting him stroke her back while their breath returned. "Wow, Zac. I don't know how you do it."

That was all she could muster to say. This unassuming man, the guy next door, secretly knew just how to please a woman. *Please her.*

Jordan didn't dare think how many women were so lucky, or could be after she'd return home. She just knew that for one last night—he was hers. Her heart could explode with the pure joy he created.

"Baby, how do you feel?"

She gazed into his gorgeous face, his eyes still brimming with lust. "Damn good."

"Perfect." Holding on to her, he backed her slowly to the far side of the tub. "Let's cool down a bit." He rose and lifted her out of the water, setting her on the three-foot wide ledge that surrounded the outside of the tub. Now dripping wet from the splashes.

Her ass rested on the wood surface, only mildly cooler than the air.

He softly kissed the palm of her hand. "Give me a second."

Jumping out of the tub, he grabbed his shorts and pulled out several condom packets. He plopped them on the wood decking and separated her legs to stand between them.

Her eyebrows lifted in question.

"What? I'm a good boy scout."

"Indeed."

Water sluiced down his abs, winding between the ridges in his six-pack and around the base of his erection. She half expected steam to rise from his skin, because the image was just too mesmerizing for his own good.

She swung her arms around his neck, impatient for his kiss, his touch.

His arms circled her, pulling her into him and deepening the kiss, taking more. After a beat, he tunneled a hand between them to caress a finger through her wet slit, and ever so gently pushed into her.

Jordan moaned into his mouth, suddenly anxious for more amazing pleasure he so expertly gave her. She was equally anxious to feel him, connect with him. The burning desire inside her that reflamed every time Zac touched her was so new. So unfamiliar, and thoroughly addicting.

"Zac, I need you."

"Lie back, baby."

She did as he bid, and he wasted no time making love to her with his mouth.

"Aah," she breathed out. She gripped his head, weaving her fingers through his hair. "Don't . . . stop."

His tongue stroked, poked inside her, and lapped at her clit. His talented mouth made her sex weep with desire. But just like last night, he wouldn't let her tip over. He kept her hanging on the edge.

"Zac."

He stood, grabbed a condom, and sheathed his swollen shaft. He stroked his bulbous tip over her, wetting himself, teasing her.

His darkened emerald eyes looked right into hers. "Turn over."

Oh yes. She lay on her stomach, and he pressed his palms against the inside of her thighs.

He rested at her entrance, and leaned over her, his chest warming her back. He laid a kiss behind her ear, and whispered, "Jordan, I think you should know, there's a chance I'm falling for you."

Without giving her a chance to process his words, he dove into her, like a man possessed.

"Oh, God, Zac." She panted. *Did he say what I think he said?* That couldn't be right. She was leaving in the morning.

His movements dominated her, consumed her, and when he hit that special spot deep inside, the tension in her core grew. He kissed and nipped at her neck and back, his breathing stronger.

At the first flutter of her orgasm, Zac increased his speed, coaxing her, building a pressure until she splintered into a million pieces.

She cried out his name.

After several more pounding strokes, he growled out her

name before collapsing on top of her. His breathing, his heartbeat, matching hers.

Still more proof of how in sync they were.

How in the hell was she going to say goodbye to him?

Chapter
TWENTY TWO

ZAC WRAPPED A soft towel around the gorgeous wet woman smiling up at him. "What?"

"You make me happy."

"I aim to please." He kissed the tip of her nose. He pulled her to standing, and guided her through the doors into the living room.

The soft carpet felt cool beneath his bare feet. His body nearly boiled in that hot tub, for all the right reasons.

"I wish my trip were longer." Jordan backed up to the bed, clutching to her towel. Her cleavage accentuated above the knot she tied at her bust made him drool. Such beautiful olive skin against the white fabric.

I agree. "Why don't you extend it?" He tried to make his voice sound more optimistic, but the very topic of her having to leave sucked the vibrance from his words.

Zac wasn't like her. Jordan was the kind of person that commanded a room the moment she entered. She exuded a confidence that made people respect her and look up to her.

Everything she did, she did with perfection. Everything she touched was excellence.

He'd been satisfied up until this point to just go with the flow.

He wanted her to stay, but how could he expect her to? She was out of his league.

Her smile faded. "If only it were that easy. I have obligations. Sam and Liddy do, too, for that matter." She smoothed her hands down his chest. "I wish I could. Because I'm going to miss you."

Why would she miss him when she could have so much more? One of those ivy-school graduates, a Wall Street exec, or some specialty doctor.

"Let's enjoy the little time we have left together," she said with a sincere smile.

"Every second." He pulled her close and kissed her, starting slowly, but soon devouring her like he hadn't just kissed her greedily outside.

She yanked on her towel, letting it fall to the carpet, then pulled herself closer into him, her beautiful hard nubs scraping along his bare chest.

When he caressed her perfectly rounded ass, she moaned into his mouth. The weight of her hips pressed her into his impatient, engorged dick and made him hungry all over again.

He whipped off the towel from his waist and laid it on the carpet. He needed her again—forever really—and couldn't bother to close the glass door to the patio. He sat on the towel, and offered her his hand.

She smiled, but didn't sit.

He knew that smile, sly and adventurous. A dirty trick waited up her sleeve. His dick stretched farther just thinking about it.

She licked her lips, went down on her knees, and instantly took him in his mouth.

"Fuck."

She fisted him with her strong, warm fingers, moving her mouth in concert with her hand. The flat of her tongue stroked his length, and the pull of her mouth nearly had him begging for mercy.

Zac gripped her head. "Jordan, I need you."

She looked up—her swollen pink lips the work of the devil. Or more like a fallen angel. But she didn't keep him waiting. Stretching for a condom in the pile he'd dropped on the floor, she ripped open the package and covered him. Taking her time, drawing out the sensation with the rubber gradually, achingly rolling over his skin.

He held out his hands as she straddled him, and slowly—so damn slowly—she lowered herself onto him.

He swore on a long breath, his eyes nearly rolling in the back of his head.

Vixen!

She moaned, and her head lobbed to the side. Her wet heat surrounded him.

A raw craving slammed into him—the deep, all-consuming longing that made him miss her even when she was right in front of him. The same rush of emotion every time she smiled at him, or laughed, or held his hand. He groaned.

She moved slowly, like she was savoring every second, and lowered her lips to his. "You drive me crazy, Zac. I can't get enough."

He cupped her cheeks. "Me, too." He wanted to say more, but what could he say? Could he profess his love for a woman he'd only just met days before? Hell no, that would scare her off. It frightened him enough just thinking about it.

Damn, but the way she ground against him, riding him senseless while her body quivered over him . . . *So not fair.* He wanted more of this.

"Zac, I think . . . there's a chance I'm falling for you, too."

Oh, Christ!

He stared into her beautiful chocolate eyes, hearing the exact words he'd said just an hour earlier. "God, Jordan." He claimed her mouth again, desire to consume every inch of her strong body.

She moved over him while never breaking contact with their precious kiss.

He wouldn't last long this time. Not with how wild she drove him.

"Watch me. I want to watch you watching me." She slid his hand from his chest, up her thigh, to her beautiful sex.

Her fingers glossed over her silky covered mons to find her sweet spot. She moved her finger slowly.

Fuck me!

Watching her touch herself in front of him had to be the most erotic thing he'd ever seen. He praised the angels above. Nothing looked more amazing than her parted mouth, that glassy lust in her eyes, combined with her sweet, little whimpers as she milked him.

"God, baby. You look so damn hot right now, pleasuring yourself while riding me."

He stroked her nipples—pulling, twisting, pinching—in just the way he learned drove her nuts.

"Oh, Zac." Her pace increased, her eyelids closed, and her head dropped back.

Even if he wasn't inside her, he would come from just the sight of this gorgeous woman on the wave of sexual ecstasy.

"Unh."

The first contractions of her pussy pulled at his dick.

He gripped her hips, supporting her, as he flexed deeper Just a few more thrusts to put him over the edge, his control tipping off the ledge of sanity. A shudder racked him from head to toe. His heart raced like ramming through a brick wall. The moment he let go, the wall exploded. He growled out her name. His hips jerked and gyrated, floating in that current of ecstasy. She screamed before collapsing to his chest, heaving equally hard as him.

He wrapped his arms around her, her body, the only hold he had on reality.

"Holy shit," she panted. "Don't let go."

Zac tightened his hold. *I won't.*

JORDAN AWOKE TO a delicious soreness, her entire body spent. She stretched, feeling the ache work through her muscles, especially her ACL. That sucker needed a deep tissue massage later.

The most glorious pain.

After they'd made love on the carpet, he grabbed some water and snacks from the mini-bar. Relaxing on the balcony, they chatted about her life in San Fran and his in New York before moving to Mexico for his grandmother. He'd said he didn't hesitate a single minute when he knew she'd needed help. And that warmed Jordan's heart, nearly bursting with pride.

How many men would do that for a loved one?

Just the idea reinvigorated her sex drive.

He'd coaxed her back inside for more delicious sex on the carpet before they went to the comfy bed.

She stared at the crystal chandelier over the bed, and grinned to herself.

Zac slept beside her, his arm curled beneath the pillow. His breathing was slow and even, his bare chest smooth in the dim light.

The urge to rub her palm along his skin was strong, but

she refrained. He looked so peaceful.

Her stomach growled. Then an idea popped in her head.

Jordan inched out bed, careful not to wake him, and quickly dressed. She scribbled a quick note on the hotel notepad in case he woke while she was gone.

Good morning, sexy. Don't move a muscle. I'll be right back.

With the hotel key in hand, she descended to the breakfast buffet with the rest of the early risers. She walked by the gym, seeing a few machines in use. Beyond the open-air lobby, even more people ran on the beach for their morning workouts. Amazing how busy the place was this early, with how hard and heavy the parties raged every night.

A salty breeze blew in from the sea. Warm and gentle.

Jordan loaded up two plates, including freshly made waffles, scrambled eggs, fruit, and bacon. She topped off the tray with orange juice glasses, and a red dahlia she picked from the bouquets behind the buffet table.

Breakfast in bed for her sexy man.

On her way back to the elevator, she passed the front desks. A line of people waited to check out, their luggage towed behind them.

Jordan's contentment dwindled slightly. Their return trip home was only a few hours away. She had no idea it would ever be this hard to walk away. The idea of leaving Zac made it difficult to swallow.

She'd actually muttered the words *I'm falling for you*

last night. She remembered it clearly. The first time she'd ever spoken those words out loud to anyone. Because everyone else prior had too many faults, too many flaws that were deal breakers in her mind. She'd never let it go further.

Zac didn't seem to have any flaws. Or they were too small to even consider as faults. Except the big one she wasn't sure anyone could get past. He lived in a foreign country.

It took the entire ride up the elevator to squash those depressive feelings back under her feet.

Enjoy the time we have left.

She slipped the key into the door, and tiptoed across the entryway. The bedroom door was still closed, leaving only a crack open. She nudged it with her foot, and found Zac still sleeping exactly where she'd left him.

Jordan set the tray on the table by the windows, then opened the sliding door to let in the breeze. Seagulls called softly in the distance, with the ever-present whooshing of the waves along the shore.

Sitting next to Zac, she delighted in the urge to caress his chest. Gentle and smooth, so as not to scare him.

He smiled, his eyes still closed, and moaned his appreciation. "*Buenos dias, querida.*"

"You look like you're having a good dream."

He opened his eyes, and held her hand over his heart. "Dream's still going."

She grinned. "Good line. I bet I can make it even better."

Zac glanced down at his crotch, and his smile curved

higher. "You just did."

Jordan giggled. "Save that for later. How about breakfast in bed first?"

He followed her gaze to the tray. "That smells amazing."

"Just for you, studly."

He pulled back the sheets to climb out of bed, his glorious member completely naked and at attention.

Jordan blushed, but didn't hide it either.

He stood full glory in front of her. "See something you like?" His devilish smirk was so irresistible.

"Yep. Every inch. Now, put him away before I get distracted." She tapped him on the ass. "I need fuel."

He chuckled, and slipped on his briefs. They sat at the table and she handed him a plate. He grabbed her feet, and draped them over his lap, lifting the red dahlia from the tray. "Nice touch." He smelled it and stuck it behind his ear. "Is red my color?"

"Sex is your color."

He laughed, and dug into the waffles.

Breakfast on the balcony overlooking the ocean with the sea breeze in her hair . . . such a sweet escape in paradise.

Zac cleared his throat. "As long as I've worked here, I've never had their breakfast."

"Well, enjoy it. I slaved for hours over it." She winked.

Everything tasted so delicious, so fresh.

He cleared his throat again, and downed half his orange juice. He scowled.

"What? Too much pulp?"

He shook his head, and coughed—then finished the orange juice in one gulp.

Jordan pulled her feet off him, and opened a bottle of water for him. "Down the wrong tube?"

In a swift move, he shoved the chair back and bolted for the mini fridge. He pulled out a can of soda, and cracked it open. After a giant swig, he gargled and spit it out in the bar sink. He repeated the action several times, sipping the soda, gargling and spitting. His face turned pale, and his lips were suddenly bright red.

"What's wrong?" Jordan's heart raced, but she kept her voice even. She'd learned never to overreact in an emergency, an important lesson as a coach if one of her athletes was ever injured.

It wasn't long before the soda can was empty. "Allergy," he croaked out. He cracked open another can, and swallowed the whole thing in a few gulps.

Holy shit. Jordan's mind whirled, panic rising in her chest.

"Do you need me to call the doctor?" She bolted over to the phone, about to dial 9-1-1. But wait, this was Mexico. *What's the emergency equivalent here?*

Zac held up his hand. "I got it," he rasped.

"Maybe they have an epi-pen or something. Shit, Zac. Tell me how to help you."

He finished the can, tossed it in the trash, then started

guzzling the water bottle she'd opened. "I only had a few bites."

"Of what? What are you allergic to?"

"Cinnamon." He gargled the water.

Jordan looked back at the plate. What in the world had cinnamon in it?

A few bites of the waffle were gone, along with the scrambled eggs.

"Waffles," he said between gulps.

Jordan scraped her hand across her forehead. She watched him very carefully, her hand over the phone, ready to call an ambulance.

He shook his head again, and his face started to return to a normal color. "I'm okay. I promise."

She finally took a deep breath, and opened another soda can. She handed it to him, her stomach in knots. "I didn't know. I'm sorry."

He took several generous sips, and sat down again. "Got my heart rate up on that one." Then he laughed. Actually *laughed*.

Jordan could only scowl at herself. And at the food in front of them, smelling delicious. Taunting them. She grabbed his plate and slid the whole thing into the trash.

"Hey, what are you doing?" he asked. "That bacon is awesome."

"It nearly killed you. *I* nearly killed you."

He sighed, his frown instant. "Don't be so dramatic."

Her eyes widened. "Dramatic?"

"It happens. I know how to handle it. Not my first fiesta."

She blinked. Then studied him. Waiting for the catch. "I can't believe you're not mad."

She rubbed her temples and paced the room, suddenly uncomfortable in her own skin.

He stopped her with his hands on her shoulders. "Jordan, I'm fine. I didn't eat that much."

"But you could have," she implored.

He sighed. "But I didn't. Do you want to finish eating?" He grabbed the bacon off her plate, and took a bite. "No big deal," he replied after swallowing.

She stared into his eyes. *How can he be so nonchalant?*

"Come sit. Eat."

He used the extra fork to stab into the fresh melon, and popped it in his mouth.

The only thing she managed to do was push the scrambled eggs around the plate. Her appetite dissolved with her earlier panic. Or perhaps with the oncoming ass-chewing she'd expected. Anytime she screwed up, there was always an ass-chewing.

It's only a matter of time. He'll find a moment to hang this over my head.

"Sorry we had to use the soda from the mini-fridge. I know that was supposed to be off limits."

He shrugged. "I'll leave him some cash. No big deal."

Her eyes narrowed again. The magic between them faded. Simply on a choked exhale. All because of some spices. She wasn't going to stick around for the lecture on what she should've done differently.

Jordan set down her fork. "I should go."

His forced optimism switched to a sad puppy dog face instantly. "Please, don't. Not because of this."

"I still have to pack. Besides, I'm . . ." Her throat hitched. "Not very good at goodbyes."

This vacation was supposed to be perfect. The connection between them had been perfect. Up until now.

Anytime the magic dies, it's time to cut and run.

Best done like ripping off a Band-Aid. No sense in elongating the pain.

She stood.

He followed, oh so close.

Damn, the man smelled just as good the morning after.

"Text me when you're on your way down. I'll help with the luggage, even drive you all to the airport."

She shook her head. "We'll call a taxi."

He swallowed, his Adam's apple moving with obvious discomfort. "Please, let me see you before you leave. I'll wait in the lobby."

Why? I only screw things up.

She couldn't make the words come out. She nodded instead.

He opened the door for her.

She moved to step out, but he pulled her back, gently by the elbow.

"Jordan. For what it's worth, you're the best time I've ever had. I meant it when I said I was falling for you."

"So did I." Her voice cracked.

Zac cupped her face, his sad smile so sweet, her knees nearly gave out.

He touched his lips to hers. Soft, tender, and equally devastating.

She pulled back and blinked away the tears. "I have to go," she whispered.

Jordan retreated to the elevator, and couldn't force herself to look at him. It took the entire ride down to stem the tears pricking her eyes.

There was a strong probability—with all the shit that went wrong during this trip—that she might never forgive herself.

Chapter
TWENTY THREE

THIS WAS ZAC'S last chance. He leaned against the stone wall under the roof of the resort's front drive, waiting for Jordan. She'd texted him and said she was on her way. He offered to help her with her luggage, but she'd declined.

She was distancing herself, and it ripped his heart from his chest.

He had no idea what to say to her, how to make her stay, to see how far this thing between them could go. The thought of watching her leave sucked the air from his body.

Finally, the women passed through the glass doors. Jordan's gaze met his, and she walked his way, tugging her suitcase behind her.

Just seeing her sent his heart racing, and his stomach in a crazy swirl. He couldn't tell whether those butterflies would make him fly or throw up.

"How are you?" she asked in a subdued voice.

When she didn't lean in to kiss his cheek, like she normally did, it cracked his heart.

"Jordan, I'm fine. I promise you. How are you?" He stroked her arms up and down.

"I'm sorry."

He grabbed her close, inhaling the sweet orange of her hair. "It was an accident. No need to apologize. Look at me."

She glanced up, mist in those beautiful brown irises.

"I'll live." He swallowed the lump in his throat. "I just . . . haven't quite figured out how I'm gonna live without you."

A tear escaped down her cheek. "Me neither."

He had so much to say, but nothing would come out. What else was he supposed to say at a time like this? As much as he wanted her to stay, looking in her sweet eyes now, he wouldn't dare ask her to give up her life in San Francisco. Her dream of coaching Olympians was there. Her closest friends were there. Going with her wasn't an option for him, his grandmother needed him. His place was in Mexico, Jordan's in Cali.

He hugged her tight and kissed her. Their last kiss.

"I'm going to miss you." He wiped another tear off her face.

Her breath was ragged. "I'm going to miss you, too."

"On your next vacation, come back."

More tears fell. She nodded. "Goodbye, Zac."

He hated to admit that he wasn't here to convince her to stay after all. Standing there, watching her climb into the taxi with her friends, he realized he'd come to say goodbye.

Goodbyes were the most painful. He'd do anything to

prevent the agony. But there was nothing he could do.

He helped the driver load in the last bag, then took the red dahlia out of his back pocket and tucked the stem into the outside compartment, with the petals hanging out. Hopefully, it would remind her of him when she got home.

The car pulled away, and he waved. Jordan didn't look back.

The bright noon sun might as well have been a downpour. A deluge in rainy season, for all it meant to him. He just watched the best thing that ever happened to him drive away.

So, this is what a broken heart feels like.

THE SADNESS AND sympathy in her friends' eyes told Jordan they knew not to ask a damn thing.

"We need to check in over here." Sam pointed and rolled her luggage in the direction of the ticket counter.

After receiving their boarding passes and clearing security, Jordan dumped her bags by their gate. "The flight's on-time, so I'm going to call my father."

"Sounds good," Liddy said, wearing another sympathetic look on her face, like pity to a hurt kitten.

So that's what my face looks like every time Liddy's nursed a broken heart. She must've hated me every time I made that face.

Jordan found an empty gate not far from the girls to

have a quiet conversation.

Her father picked up after the first ring. "Beck residence."

"Hi, Dad."

"Hey, Jordan. How was the trip? Did you ladies have fun?"

"It was fine. I just want to make sure you'll be at the airport at four-thirty."

"Yes, of course." He paused. "Jordan, what's wrong? You don't sound right."

She paused to gather her thoughts. Did she really want to explain what happened, to her father, no less? She glanced at her watch. "Dad, this trip didn't go as smoothly as our last one."

"What happened?" His voice was clipped.

"Everyone is fine . . ."

"But?"

She cringed. "But . . . a bartender drugged Liddy, and ransacked our room."

"What?" he barked.

"I told you, everyone is okay. Liddy is perfectly fine. Let me finish, please."

Silence.

Jordan continued. "He was caught and arrested." *Thank the heavens above for Zac.* "We found out there was a whole string of these incidents at the resort the last few months. But we got everything back."

"Uh huh. Then what?" Her father's voice was calmer, but still held that tinge of anger.

She took a deep breath. "Then I served a cinnamon waffle to the man who caught the bartender, only to learn he's allergic to cinnamon."

The line was eerily quiet.

Oh shit. Here it comes.

"Jordan, the man could have gone into anaphylaxis and died."

"I know," she replied timidly. "But he's fine."

The heavy sigh on the other end of the line was the trigger. The same sigh he always gave before the lecture. "I am at a loss what to say. You put your friend in danger. You put the man who saved her in danger. This is pure negligence. Don't you know not to drink things a stranger gives you? Basic protection skills. How could you have let something like this happen?" His voice rose with every statement.

"I've been asking myself that same question."

"And?" He controlled his anger, but just barely.

Tears welled in her eyes. She didn't know how to respond other than *yes sir*.

"We can talk about this more when you get home. You must decide how you'll conduct yourself in life. Will you be present and in the moment? Or will you let life take you wherever the hell it wishes, stealing your goals and dreams? Mistakes likes these can cost you your chance at Olympic coaching."

Another pause. *There's always more.*

"I'll be waiting outside baggage claim." The line went dead.

A sob escaped. She slammed a hand over her mouth, and turned toward the window so no one would see. Tears streamed incessantly down her cheeks. Why did she even bother putting on makeup that morning?

Her father was right. She allowed this to happen—all of it—because of her negligence. As the organizer of the whole trip, she was the one responsible. She should've been more aware. She *knew* better.

Jordan escaped to the closest bathroom, washed her face, and put herself back together as best she could. She just needed to get home, get the berating over with, and erase all the memories of Puerto Vallarta from her head.

All of them.

Including the beautiful ones of the man that stole her heart, and for once made her feel what unconditional love with a partner might be like.

SAM'S STARE WAS too intrusive when Jordan returned to the gate.

"You told him, didn't you?" her friend asked.

Jordan cleared the tears from her throat. "He'll wait for us at baggage claim." She plopped herself down in her seat, and started playing a game on her phone. Anything other than look Sam in the eye.

Sam set down a bridal magazine she'd brought with her. "This is not your fault."

"I know."

"You clearly don't."

Liddy sighed, obviously annoyed. "If anyone has the right to be angry, it's me. And I'm not. So when we get there, I'll talk to him. Tell him to back off."

Jordan snorted. "Good luck with that." She opened her purse, and pulled out the red dahlia she'd found sticking out of her luggage. Her throat closed in on itself again.

Her memento of paradise. Of perfection. No doubt it would be dead by morning. Much like her sweet escape in Mexico.

"What are you the most upset by?" Sam asked bluntly. "Your dad's berating you for something you had no control over, or leaving Zac?"

Jordan scowled. "I've said it from the very beginning. This was a *vacation*. No relationship can come from a fling like this."

Sam laughed and threw her magazine in Jordan's lap.

"What is wrong with you?"

"Did you really just say that? To *me*? I'm living proof that's bullshit."

She tossed the magazine back.

"Were those not my *exact words* in Santa Cruz? And how did I meet Chase?" She flashed her engagement ring.

"Vacation flings are the best kind. They see you at your best."

Jordan felt like throwing up. "Exactly the opposite. Zac saw me at my worst. When I nearly killed him."

"First," Sam held up that signature finger. "That is *not* your worst. Stomach flu or hospital bed take precedence over that. Second, even if it were at your worst, he still wanted to be with you. That's when you know it's *real*."

"Major difference between Chase and *this*." Jordan sat up, and gestured to the airport. "Zac is not a one-hour car ride from home and can telecommute. He lives in a *different country*. Besides," Jordan plopped back against her seat like an angsty teenager, "I doubt he's interested in settling on someone who nearly killed him."

Sam rolled her eyes. "You are such a drama queen right now. You're normally the overly optimistic cheerleader."

"What do you expect?" Liddy chimed in. "She just talked to her dad. She always gets like this when her father's around."

Jordan exhaled and slumped further in her seat. Thoughts raced through her head of the conversation with her father. Even conversations from years passed replayed like old MASH episodes. Grainy, and irritatingly relevant.

"Why do I feel like I keep going through this?"

Sam leaned in close and lowered her voice. "The perfectionist stuff really rubbed off on you. Countless times he only showed his approval and affection when you won. First place, or straight As, whatever. If you got second place, or missed curfew by a minute, that wasn't good enough."

God, Jordan couldn't count the number of times her father had hounded her ass. It was more than raising the bar or pushing her to be all she could be. He had unrealistic expectations. It was almost like her failure was a direct reflection on him.

How had she not realized this?

In her thirty years, she couldn't remember a time when her father wasn't either berating her for a failure or praising her for a success. *Only* successes. Two extremes and no middle ground.

Liddy leaned forward, meeting her gaze head-on, breaking her stream of thought. "You now treat all your romantic relationships the same way. On a conditional basis. The second something fails to live up to your expectations, either you or the other person, it must not be real love. You feel like you can't trust *unconditional* love."

The thought was like a thunk between the eyes. "When did you become Dr. Phil?"

Liddy shrugged. "Could be side effects of the meds, or it could be that I'm a closet genius, hiding my gifts from the both of you for years just for moments like this. When I'd make *sure* you were paying attention."

They laughed because it felt good, releasing the tension, even if just for a minute. She knew what awaited her return, and she was none too thrilled.

But Liddy's last revelation stayed on her mind like an

overplayed advertisement.

Do I really have a problem trusting unconditional love?

Chapter
TWENTY FOUR

ZAC SAT NUMBLY for he couldn't say how long in the kitchen, waiting for the minutes to tick by before work. That's all he dared himself to think about, work. Maybe he could pick up a few extra shifts in the scuba shop this week. Hell, even cleaning out the training pool, a job he normally hated. Anything to keep his mind off *her*.

Of course, in reality, Jordan's smile, her laugh, her sexy flirting, even the smell of her sunscreen haunted him.

He stared out the window, watching his grandma tend her garden. He couldn't sit out back anymore either. That place held a special memory he couldn't take right now. That spectacular, toe-curling, head-spinning memory.

After a short time, his grandmother shuffled through the back door to the kitchen sink to wash her hands. "Zachary, *niñito*, are you going to tell me what's on your mind, or have me guess?"

He shrugged.

"Is it the sweet girl you met?"

"If you already know the answer, why do you ask?"

Gram patted his wrist, and washed her hands. "Did she leave?"

He nodded.

"What a shame. I really liked her. Sweet and smart. Where does she live?"

"San Francisco."

Her eyes lit up. "Oh, I love San Francisco. You could always go up there and see her. Have you ever been there?"

He shook his head. "She's not interested in a long distance relationship."

She smiled. "I think you'd love it. Perhaps you should surprise her."

"Gram, you don't surprise women like that now-a-days. I'd get arrested for stalking."

Hell if he hadn't already thought of that. All his time spent tending bar, he'd managed to stash away some money, so that wasn't the issue. He was her vacation fling—the girls said as much the first time they'd met. Someone like Jordan doesn't spend her life with the likes of Zac. He wasn't gonna kid himself.

"I'm too tired to cook tonight, so let's just have leftovers, *si?*"

"Okay."

He didn't expect Gram to cook for him. He never really had, but she'd said she loved it. Gave her purpose. Aside from her garden and a handful of close friends, he was her reason for living, so she'd claimed.

He helped her dish up their leftovers on plates, then pulled out her chair at the table.

"You love the girl, don't you? She really seemed to love you back."

On a deep breath, he sat and just stared at his food. "Not enough, apparently. Doesn't matter, I guess. I don't have much to offer."

Her fork clanked on the dish, and her smile was gone. If he didn't know any better, he might have thought she was glaring at him. "Don't ever say such nonsense again. You'll ruin my perfectly good day. Just planted two new orchids to go with my cherubs out back."

"*Lo siento.*"

She took several bites of the leftover enchiladas, and her smile returned.

"I'm glad to see you working in the garden again," he said.

"It's so peaceful back there. But it wears me out faster than it used to."

"I know. How about I pick up a few ferns on my way home from work tonight. I'll plant them this weekend for you."

Her expression turned serious as she studied him. "I'm sorry about Jordan, sweetheart. She seemed like quite a catch."

He nodded. There was no point in hiding his depression.

Not from *abuelita*. "Yeah, I thought so, too."

"But don't talk down about yourself like that. She'd be the luckiest woman in the world to have you at her side. Because women don't need money or possessions to be happy. At least, not any woman worth having. What women appreciate the most is your support, love, and laughter. All three of which you have in spades, my dear. As long as she gives you her love and support, whomever she may be. Then you have my blessing."

Zac held his grandmother's hand. "No woman could live up to you."

She waved away the comment like swatting a fly, her cheeks pink. "You work tonight, no?"

"Yes." As much as he could until Jordan became a distant memory.

"*Bueno.* Finish your dinner before you head out. I'm going to bed early. Long day. Beautiful, but long."

When she finished her food, Grandma stood, and kissed him on the forehead.

He cleaned up the kitchen, and dressed for work. By the time he needed to leave, Gram was fast asleep in bed. He tiptoed into her room, and kissed her on the top of her white curls.

"See you in the morning," he whispered.

The shift that night was the same as most others, with countless guests partying and drinking into the wee hours of the morning. Simon worked beside him, neither of them in a talkative mood. Tips were less than normal, but he didn't care. The light in paradise had dwindled ever since a livewire from San Francisco had taken the energy with her back home.

Four in the morning, Zac returned home. His normal routine, with the keys on the coffee table. He checked on his grandmother, still sleeping softly in bed. A little smile graced her face. Good dreams tonight.

Zac was grateful for that.

What women appreciate most is your support, love, and laughter.

All three of which, she'd given him without pause. And as a child, all three had saved his life. *She* had saved his life.

"You're right, *abuelita,*" he whispered. "Sweet dreams."

Chapter
TWENTY FIVE

JORDAN'S FATHER BROODED beside his car outside the airport, waiting for the girls to arrive. His signature scowl made him look older than he really was, even though he had a full head of black hair. His tan skin from Venezuelan genes looked more weathered than when she'd left.

"*Hola, mija,*" he grunted.

She kissed him on each cheek.

He wordlessly took their luggage and stacked them in the back of his SUV, scowl still firmly in place.

Big surprise.

To his credit, he didn't bring up the phone conversation from earlier. Instead, her friends filled the dead air with chatter about the trip—shopping, hiking, dancing, and wonderful food.

In which Jordan barely participated. The impending conversation with her father was all she could think about.

How is it that I let it go on this long? I'm an adult, a grown woman, and he still treats me like a fifteen-year-old?

At what point will he just say, I'm so sorry, that must be hard. *At what point will he trust me to be an adult? He just keeps judging me.*

The more she thought, the clearer everything became. Her friends were right. She'd become what she despised—a coward. All the partying in college and bouncing from one casual relationship to the next wasn't rebelling, as she'd thought. It was running. Really, all that recklessness had gotten her nowhere.

Her father drove through the city, dropping Sam and Liddy off at Liddy's house. Her father unloaded the car with their bags, setting them right beside the door, while her friends each gave her a fortifying hug.

She needed it.

"Call me when you're through." Sam gave her an extra squeeze. "I can come over with some wine."

"Ladies," her father interrupted. "Be sure to drink lots of water. Hydration is important after travel. Especially you, Lydia." He gave her a knowing look.

"Thanks, Mr. B. I got it from here," she replied.

Her friend smiled, but Jordan easily spotted the mild irritation.

"Jordan, let's go. Your mother is waiting."

She climbed into the vehicle and mustered her courage. Enough time had passed for her not to realize how much her father's baggage affected her.

"Dad, please drop me at home. I'll unpack and come

over for dinner, so we can talk."

Her father's eyes widened infinitesimally, but he nodded.

She wiped her palms against her shorts. Having a few hours to prepare herself would have to do. Then, there was no turning back.

JORDAN WALKED THROUGH her parents' front door and headed straight for the kitchen. Taking the time to think about what she wanted to say resulted in one resounding theme. *This is my father's baggage.*

She had no explanation why he was still so strict and critical of her, even after she'd moved out on her own. Likely he'd learned it from his parents. But this couldn't keep up any longer.

"Hi, Mom."

"Baby, you're home. I heard about your trip. I am so glad everyone's okay." Her mother's warm arms pulled her into an embrace, and it was all Jordan could do not to fall to the floor in a big mess.

"Wasn't as big a deal as Dad probably made it out to be," Jordan replied. "You know how he gets. How was your week?" Changing the subject only delayed the inevitable—standing up to one's stubborn Venezuelan father required extra fortitude.

"Busy. I'm making *arepas*, his favorite. To help soften his mood."

"Smart." *I'll take all the help I can get.*

Her father was upset with her, and she had to confront him. She'd fallen in love with a man in Puerto Vallarta whom she'd chased away. Suddenly life had lost all its sparkle.

"Where is he?"

Her mother nodded to the patio door. "Out back."

Her father sat on an Adirondack chair, sipping a beer. He glanced her way. "Jordan, take a seat."

Her heart raced. But oh no, she would be the one in control of this conversation.

"Dad, before you start. Let me say something." She pulled the other chair in front of him, and sat so that he had nowhere else to look but at her. "I've given this a lot of thought."

He lifted a single eyebrow.

She bit the inside of her cheek, but didn't stop. She couldn't stop. If she didn't hit this head-on, when would it end? It was about damn time she stood up for herself.

"Our conversation on the phone at the airport upset me. It got me thinking how many *discussions* over my lifetime we've had like that." She inhaled a shaky breath. "I need you to treat me like an adult."

He blinked. "*Perdon?*"

"I'm not a child anymore. I don't need you to solve all my problems. You've berated me my whole life, whether I screwed up a vault, got a B on a test, or overflowed the toilet. Your judgment has ripped me apart."

He tried to say something, and she put up her hand.

God, it felt good.

"I've always taken it. Because I know you mean well, and have the best intentions. The problem is now any mistake I make, I hear your criticizing words in my head, even if you're not around. I can't live like that anymore."

His scowl deepened and his fingers tightened around the bottle.

Keep going, he has to hear all of it.

"I'm an adult. It's time for you trust me to be one. If I screw up, so be it. They're my mistakes from which to learn. If I ask for advice, you can give me your honest opinion. But the way you treat me, and talk to me like a toddler, is tearing us apart, and it can't go on. Please know, I appreciate your concern, and I love you. But this is *my* life. And I'm happy with my life. I need you to respect me and my choices."

She let out the last bit of breath she held in.

He stared in silence for several long minutes.

Say something.

Eventually, he set his beer on the side table. "You think I berate you?" His voice softened.

"Yes."

He nodded.

She waited patiently; she'd given him a lot to process.

Her mother stood just inside the patio door, and watched. Her expression mirrored much of her father's. Confusion. Concern. It's like they both held their breath waiting for him to explain in finite detail why he couldn't back off.

"Well," he finally started, "I can't make any promises about my behavior, except to say I'll try and butt out."

She sat up and fidgeted in her chair, not sure she heard him right.

He ran a hand down the back of his neck. "Jordan, I only want the best for you. Perhaps I was overbearing at times, but I love you. I've always been proud of you."

She sat speechless.

"When you told me someone had drugged your friend and robbed you all, it took all my discipline not to fly down there and kick the shit out of the man who did that to you. I'm sorry if my frustration came out on you."

She grabbed his hand, and squeezed. "You didn't have to. He got his ass kicked already." *By the same man I gave my heart to, and subsequently left behind.*

"You're my little girl. You always will be, no matter your age. I will always feel protective."

"I appreciate that. You and mom raised me right. So, you don't have to be so protective anymore." She smiled. "I got this."

Her father smiled at the phrase she'd always used at gymnastics meets to pump herself up for a tough routine. It was a phrase he'd always chanted from the sidelines. *You've got this.*

"I'm glad you're home. Despite all that drama on your

trip, I hope you had some fun."

Her smile slipped. The memory of Zac was still so fresh. So heartbreaking. "Honestly, it was the best time of my life."

He looked at her strangely. As if he could see through her heartache. "I hope so."

"Dinner is ready," her mother called. "Quick, before it gets cold."

Chapter TWENTY SIX

ZAC WOKE THE next morning to a quiet house. All the lights were still off, but the sunlight through the windows brightened the room easily enough. *"Abuelita?"* he called. *Strange for her to still be sleeping.*

In the kitchen, everything was in its place. The kettle was cold. She hadn't made her morning tea.

He maneuvered down the hallway to her bedroom.

The door was slightly ajar, just the way she normally kept it at night.

Zac nudged it open, and peered inside.

His grandmother lay in bed, a pillow tucked in the crook of her arm. Just as he'd left her when he'd come home from work.

Yesterday must have really wiped her out.

He stepped back, letting her sleep.

Before he moved a few feet away, he stopped.

In the exact same position.

His heart froze.

He went back into the room, holding his breath. He touched her hand.

Cold.

"*Abuelita*?" he whispered.

He felt for a pulse in her wrist, and watched her chest for a rise and fall.

Nothing.

No pulse, no breath.

He felt her neck, searching for the artery. Her skin was ice. "Grandma," he barked.

Nothing.

"No!" Zac gently opened one of her eyes. Her pupil didn't dilate. "Eva! Wake up!"

His hands trembled as he started CPR. Deep down, he knew it was pointless. She'd been gone for hours with how cold she was. But he wouldn't stop. He couldn't.

Not after how hard she fought her cancer. How hard she fought for him during his treatments. Not after everything they'd been through.

"Eva!" He bellowed between compressions, fighting back tears.

Not now, please.

He choked down the sobs long enough to call for an ambulance and then resumed compressions. Her frail body didn't react at all.

By the time the ambulance arrived, Zac was out of breath and his arms ached. The paramedics took over and tried their best.

"*Lo siento, señor. Esta muerta.*"

He scraped his forehead with the heels of his hands. *This can't be happening.*

The man started speaking to him about taking her remains to the funeral home, something about procedure, would call in a few days, blah blah. None of it processed in his mind. He couldn't take his gaze off his *abuelita*.

So tiny in the bed. All cold and frail.

The paramedic grabbed his shoulder. "She went peacefully in her sleep. We should all be so lucky."

The man's words provided no comfort. "I was extremely lucky," Zac replied, "to have her in my life."

"Is there anyone you want us to call for you?"

Zac wiped his eyes, and shook his head. "No. I'll do it."

He sat numbly as the man's words floated in the air meaninglessly. "You're a good man . . . That kind of love is rare."

Zac was shattered into a million pieces. He'd lost two women he'd loved the most in one week. One damn week. Fate had played some kind of cruel joke on him.

One Week Later

ZAC'S TIE DANGLED loose around his neck, and suit coat in his hand felt as heavy as his heart. His grandmother's house was too quiet. Too dim, despite the afternoon sun basking the living room in light.

He tossed his car keys on the coffee table, along with the rest of the funeral cards.

His phone dinged with a text. From his mother.

Grabbing dinner to bring back to the house. What do you want?

He shoved the phone in his pocket.

His parents and sisters had come in for the funeral, though Zac had made all the arrangements. His mother used the same tactic during depressing times—feed everyone. Food solved everything in a crisis. A trait she learned from his *abuelita*.

But Zac had lost all his appetite.

Lost more than that.

He plopped down on the couch, dreading going through her things. Shelf after shelf held countless St. Mary figurines and other trinkets she'd collected. How could he bear to throw out a single one? They held all of her prayers.

He grabbed a photo album from the side table, and scanned the images of Gram and her husband, Ernesto. They'd taken so many trips together. She'd loved to travel until her health had failed. He flipped a page, and stared at her smiling face, in front of the Golden Gate bridge. She hugged Ernesto, her young image so full of life.

A note under the picture read, "If I ever move back to the States, I'll retire in San Francisco."

Tears pricked his eyes. He closed the book and put it back. There was no way he could do this now. His parents were due any second. Maybe they could tackle that chore, because he just couldn't bear it.

He had to do something. Sitting in an empty house would drive him insane. He changed out of his suit into shorts and a T-shirt and headed out back. He turned on the spigot to water Grandma's garden. A few plants had started to wilt. He gave them all a good soak, checking the soil like Eva had taught him. She'd tan his hide if he let a single plant die. He smiled even as a tear ran down his cheek.

"Gram, I miss you," he whispered to the universe.

He walked as he sprayed more plants, trying not to look. The cushioned loveseat taunted him. *The* wicker loveseat. The flowers in the arch hadn't wilted at all—the pink blooms were just as bright as before.

His chest caved. He was forced to sit. The hose kept going, forming a large puddle in the grass.

He'd lost both Jordan and his grandmother.

He had nothing to show for his life. No real career, no possessions.

Definitely not worthy of Jordan's love. The woman was nearly an *Olympian.* The very definition of the best in her field. The cream of the crop, and so driven.

What in the world would she see in me? She's probably already forgotten the connection we had.

Chapter
TWENTY SEVEN

THE RELENTLESS KNOCKING on Jordan's front door woke her from the couch. She'd apparently fallen asleep at some point watching the Lifetime channel.

Jordan stood and opened the door.

Sam, in her linen pants and gray tank top, looked like she was on her way to a meeting.

"Good, you're still alive." She stepped in, and wrapped Jordan in a hug. "You haven't been answering your phone."

"I was sleeping."

Sam eyed her. "I drove by the gym, thinking you were coaching your normal afternoon littles over the summer. When I didn't see you, I thought maybe you were sick or something."

"I'm not coaching this summer."

Sam dropped her bag. "Are you kidding? Since when?"

Jordan plopped back down on the couch. "Since we got back from Mexico." Just saying the name of the country felt raw on her throat.

Sam's movements grew very slow, like entering the den of a lioness. She lowered herself to the couch next to her. "You *always* coach club team in the summer. Something is really wrong."

Jordan sighed. "I'm okay. I needed a break." That was a partial truth, the other part was she needed to find a way to get out of her funk.

A new show came on the Lifetime channel. Something involving a small town and a busty redhead.

"The *Lifetime* channel?" Sam gasped. "Oh, no. Not you. Get up." She grabbed the remote and turned off the television.

"What?"

"You're coming with me to the spa. They have a luxury place on the fifteenth floor skyrise by the bay. I'll call Liddy, too."

Jordan sighed, her whole body a boneless pile of mush. "I don't have the energy."

"Tough. Get up. You're not doing this. I will not let you shut yourself out. Lifetime is the last straw. You *hate* that cliché."

Jordan shrugged a shoulder. "I can see the appeal, now."

"Get up. Go throw on your workout clothes, and I'll spring for a foot rub."

Sam yanked on her arm, and finally got her ass off the couch. Not long after, all three ladies were in their own pedicure chairs. Liddy's makeup was flawless, having just come from work at the designer boutique she managed. Sam was a natural beauty on her own, and never needed much. Jordan couldn't have cared less if her face was washed, let alone covered in makeup. It had been a week since leaving Mexico, the same amount of time she'd gone without makeup.

"I'm so proud of you," Sam announced after Jordan recounted the conversation with her father. "That's been a long time coming."

"I finally realized I'd never actually said anything to him about the way he made me feel. I always just took it. But at thirty years old . . . yeah, time to end that mentality."

"Has he stuck to his word?" Liddy asked. "Has he backed off at all?"

Jordan frowned. "There's hasn't been much to intrude on the last week." She winced when the technician dug into an especially tight spot in her calf.

"About that. Why'd you stop coaching?" Liddy asked.

"I'm still coaching my high schoolers, just not the summer club."

"You love the littles. Does this have anything to do with Zac?"

Jordan closed her eyes, and leaned her head against the cushion. Even hearing his name hurt.

Liddy always cut straight through the BS to the heart of everything. Of course, Liddy was the kind to watch Lifetime movies non-stop after breakups. Sam and Jordan were always there to pull her out of it. This was the first time Jordan needed them to do that for her.

"You really cared about him." Sam's voice turned softer.

I guess I did. She'd never been hung up on a relationship after it ended like this—if she could call what she and Zac had a relationship.

They finished their pedicures, and the manager escorted them to the upper balcony where they served mimosas, pastries, and finger sandwiches.

The warm breeze overlooking the bay reminded Jordan a little of the executive suite back at the resort. Her cheeks heated remembering that hot tub.

"Ooh, look!" Liddy leaned forward in her chair at the iron patio table. "They have a kite festival going on."

Jordan peered over the railing at the park fifteen floors below. Countless people mingled in the grassy area, with over thirty kites of various colors and shapes catching the wind. "It's a good day for that."

She sank back in her chair, and guzzled half the mimosa.

"I've never seen you hung up on a guy like this." Sam grabbed another one for her from a passing waitress.

Jordan nodded. "I know. Not gonna lie, I'm not a fan of it."

"What makes Zac so different?"

She stared at her plate of canapes and thought about the answer to that question over and over. He'd suffused her mind and body with a satisfaction she hadn't known she craved. She rapidly blinked back the tears. "I don't know. With him, I just felt . . . alive. As much as I hate to admit it, because we're all women and gung-ho to lead our own lives, he had that humble, white knight mentality that I just found so endearing. A man who loves his grandmother enough to give up his life and take care of her . . . "

Liddy nodded. "You said he survived cancer as a child, too, right?"

Her heart cinched. "Yeah."

"That certainly puts life into perspective."

"I'll admit," Jordan interjected. "The idea of someone moving to Mexico to be a full-time bartender, I thought at first that he was escaping life. No real motivation to do more. How judgmental and a snobbish of me. But now I can say with all honesty, that was the old me."

Her friends smiled.

"And another thing," she continued, "Zac was luckier than most adults I know. He found his peace in life early. Granted, forced into it a bit with cancer, but he made the most of his situation. Other than Sam's Chase, who else has found that real balance in life, and *lives* it every day?"

"I think *that's* what you love most about Zac." Sam's expression turned somber.

Jordan closed her eyes and pictured him so clearly in her mind, that easy smile, the carefree look in his eyes.

"Other than the sex, of course," Liddy added.

Sam laughed.

Jordan's face flushed with heat.

"So, what are you going to do about him?"

"What can I do, Liddy?" She let out a heavy sigh. "I wouldn't dream of asking him to leave his grandmother. Nor can I abandon my athletes. Two of them have Olympic potential."

Her friends remained silent as they watched her process her thoughts.

Because what she was going to say next hurt too damn much.

She gripped the arm rest. "I lost him." *Simple as that.*

Liddy frowned.

"But I learned so much about myself on that trip. I learned how to trust myself. I have him to thank for it."

Sam reached out and grabbed her hand. "You learned that you can't love people in slices. It's the whole pie, the good and bad, including the inconvenient."

Her breath was shaky, but she was at least able to smile. For the first time in a week. "I did that, didn't I? Compartmentalized people. Felt like I wasn't worthy of someone's love unless I'd won a gold medal first. Been perfect across the board."

"There's no such thing as perfect," Liddy replied. "Just what's perfect for you."

"Screw-ups are all part of it, too." Sam winked. "You know I'm an expert in that."

She blinked back a tear, and watched the kites dance in the breeze.

"The next time love comes around—if I'm lucky enough for a second chance—I won't give up on it. I'll get back up on the balance beam, and trust myself."

"Trust *him*, too." Sam held up her mimosa for a toast. "Because that's what love is. Trust."

Liddy and Jordan clinked their glasses with hers.

The tart drink was strong and exactly what she needed.

"Oh! I forgot." Jordan reached into her purse, and pulled out the necklaces she'd bought in Mexico. "I have gifts for you. A little keepsake from our vacation."

"You didn't have to do that." Sam set down her glass.

"I meant to give these to you right after I bought them, but then . . ." She gave them the boxes, keeping the third one for herself.

The women opened their gifts, the purple flower pendant for Liddy, and the orange one for Sam.

Liddy grinned. "This is stunning! Where did you find this?"

"Glass shop in Yelapa. I saw these, and just knew you'd love them. I have a blue one for me."

Sam leaned across her chair and hugged Jordan. "You're so thoughtful, sweetie. I love it. Thank you."

"I love you ladies, too. Every single slice."

Chapter
TWENTY EIGHT

FOUR LONG WEEKS of hell. There was no other way to describe it—four long weeks since Jordan had walked out of his life and his grandmother had died.

Zac moped around the house. All the boxes stacked by the door were full of her personal things that his mother wanted. He was going to ship them out this weekend, so at least then he might be able to breathe beyond the depression.

Most of the shelves were empty, save for a few trinkets and the figurines that none of the family had wanted. He didn't have the heart to throw them away. Or pack them away either.

Even his boss noticed how badly this affected him. The man kept offering him time off. No, he did not need time off. Dammit! Zac needed to *do* something.

Jordan's face, her laugh, her scent, invaded his thoughts constantly. He dreamt about her every night. He was borderline batshit crazy at this point.

Add to that all the questions that ran through his head that weighed him down—should he sell the house? His grandmother had left the property to him in her will, and he had the finances for the upkeep and taxes, but the place was more than he needed. Maybe he'd be happier in a one-bedroom apartment? Closer to the resort, or perhaps open up his own dive shop? Or should he just move back to New York, closer to his parents and sisters?

He snorted. *What the hell would I do back there?*

Of course, the thought of going to San Francisco popped into his head more than once. Each time, he'd ruled it out just as quickly.

In the time since Jordan had left, he'd heard from her once, texting him that she was home safely, and "thank you for the flower."

Nothing more, nothing less.

He pinched the bridge of his nose. Again, he couldn't blame her. They both knew she was out of his league.

Suddenly, the sound of a large truck rumbling down the street caught his attention.

Shit! The garbage!

He'd forgotten to put the trash out last week, not that it was much, but it started to stink. He grabbed the bag he'd left on the back patio and ran through the house out the front door.

The truck had already passed, and had reached the neighbors.

Damn.

The guy stopped, and waved him over.

"*Gracias,*" he puffed out.

"*De nada.*"

Zac walked back toward the house, stopping to retrieve the letters from the mailbox. Something else he'd consistently forgotten as of late.

Zac, get it together.

He dropped the mail on the counter and slumped into Grandma's chair at the table, tossing bills in one pile, sympathy cards in another, and junk straight into the recycle bin. A colorful glossy oversized card caught his eye.

The glass shop in Yelapa.

The card showcased several pictures of glass pieces, some he recognized from their tour a month ago. He flipped the card over.

There, staring back at him, was the big blue wave Jordan had loved. He could see why—various shades of blue with "foam" layered across the top was a masterpiece by any standard. His finger stroked down the card along the crest of the wave, as if he could feel the precise edges and the craftsmanship.

The ache in his gut intensified.

He dropped the offending card in the recycling bin, along with the rest of the junk. The more times he thought of her, the more splinters his heart cracked into. The fractals relished in stabbing him in the middle of the night, keeping him from sleeping. He had to stop this self-torture.

He stomped up the stairs to his bedroom to shower and get ready for work. Some people could take it one day at a time. He had to take it minute by minute.

ZAC PLANTED THE last green ferns in the backyard garden. The ones he'd promised his grandmother he'd buy. He watered the new additions with a good soak and then stood back to survey the green space.

The flowers were in full bloom, and the fragrances so beautiful. The jasmine bush flourished by the arbor.

He couldn't sell this place. Ever. This was his *abuelita's* life's work. So many memories in this garden, so much love.

But staying here was out of the question, too. He needed to move on with life. He'd rent the place out to vacationers, or a nice family. To someone who would appreciate the oasis the way his gram did.

He had no idea what he was going to do. His mom urged him to move back to New York, but that wasn't home. Not anymore.

He didn't have to figure it out right now. For today, he had another shift at the resort. This weekend would be packed with guests going scuba diving, and he told Joaquin he'd help.

Zac hopped in his car, and drove down the hill toward the bay. Nothing on the radio was any good, so he switched over to satellite radio.

Prince's "Little Red Corvette" blared over the speakers.

He smiled. He just couldn't help it. As much as this song hurt to hear, Jordan's face was so vibrant in his memory. How alive she was in his arms as he spun her on that dance floor. How alive she made him feel.

He rolled around the next bend, and spotted a new billboard ad going up. The workers stretched the vinyl canvas across the wooden display.

For the glass shop.

Zac pulled the car over to the shoulder. Then sat and stared at the sign.

A literal and figurative sign.

How many times would the universe have to punch him in the gut until he got the message?

"I hear you," he said aloud. "You stubborn spirit guide. Or is that a persistent *abuela*?" He grinned.

This is what they call a fork in the road, Zac.

The vicious grip on his heart all these weeks had been love. He missed Jordan, but he had no way to know if she missed him back. A lot could've happened in a month; she could have moved on, found someone new. Hell, she'd probably forgotten his name already.

His teeth sunk into his upper lip.

Or she could be dreaming about him every night, just like he had of her. She could be pining for him, wishing for a way to be together. The chance alone . . . what if he never took it? He'd spend his whole life wondering.

"You swore 'no what-ifs,' Zac," he convinced himself. "Go for it, and see where what-if can lead."

He pulled back onto the road and drove to the resort. After a quick conversation with his boss, he accepted the time off. He couldn't say for how long exactly. It all depended on one critical conversation, if he wasn't too late.

His hands went slick.

He drove home and packed a bag. Unchartered territory had never scared him so much in his life, except for once when he sat in that hospital unsure if he'd survive. Even this might rival that fear.

For the first time in as long as he could remember, Zac had a plan. He wanted something so badly, he was willing to move heaven and earth. He knew in his gut, if he didn't at least try, he'd regret it.

He tossed the bag in the car and searched his mobile app for the next flight out. But first, he had one more stop to make.

Chapter
TWENTY NINE

JORDAN'S BUZZER ECHOED across her apartment walls. She set down the water pitcher from watering the new dahlia flowers she'd bought. Two pots now graced her tiny back patio.

She opened the door, and gasped. "Zac?"

"Am I too late?" There he stood, his gorgeous green eyes glittering with hope. His V-neck powder-blue T-shirt hung loose around his frame. Casual chic in jeans and leather-sole shoes.

Her mouth had gone dry and her heart skipped a beat. She gripped the door handle, unable to move. "Too late? For what?"

"I brought you something." He dug into his backpack, and pulled out a paper-wrapped bundle. "A . . . memento, if you will."

She absently put out her hands to take the gift, but couldn't stop staring into his eyes. "Come in. How did you find me?" She stepped back, and he crossed her threshold.

His exotic cologne hit her just right—instantly sending her back to their night in the hot tub. The same scent that made her knees weak and her senses blur.

"Found you on social media. Then looked you up online."

Jordan blinked. She'd been a mess of a human being the last week, and hadn't touched her social media accounts since before her trip. There was no point. She was sure he'd lost all interest.

She watched him carefully as he looked around her small apartment. A half-wall separated the kitchen and dinette from the living room, a cozy space with cream colored sofas accented with blue and purple pillows, and matching valances.

He set his backpack on the floor beside the whitewashed coffee table.

Is that everything he brought with him to California?

"This is so you." He motioned to the apartment, which he could probably walk across in five steps.

"It's what my salary can afford, close to the school." *Why does my voice sound so airy?*

"I love it." Zac took a shaky breath. "God, you look just as amazing."

Her heart skipped. *So do you.* But she didn't have enough air in her lungs to say the words.

"I'm just gonna take a giant leap here, and go for it. If I crash and burn . . . " He bit his lip, the trepidation on his face as thick as her tongue. Swollen at the realization that Zac stood in her living room. *Her* Zac.

"I love you." He blurted his confession, followed by a hesitant smile. "This month apart has been agony. I've never wanted a woman this much in my life. I've never wanted to take a chance this big before. I'm the kind of guy that goes with the flow, and enjoys the easy life. Then you swooped into my world, this incredibly driven, motivated woman who literally flips circles around me. Intimidating as hell, and yet I can't resist. I'm all in."

Jordan couldn't breathe. She set the heavy package on the table, for fear she'd drop it. Her hands started tingling the second he began to speak. Her stomach somersaulted over and over again, a thousand steps beyond butterflies.

Is this what real love feels like?

"I know I haven't accomplished that much in my life," he continued, filling her silence. "Compared to you, I must seem like a freeloader or something, but I promise I want this chance with you. You have every ounce of my heart, and I'll spend every waking moment making you happ—"

Jordan threw her arms around his shoulders and crushed her lips against his.

He grunted mid-word, and gripped her back.

God, he felt like heaven.

She couldn't taste him fast enough. The need was too great to bear. He tasted like mint and whiskey. She could barely breathe. If he didn't kiss her back, she'd faint.

She dived deeper into his mouth, hoping she would taste the salty ocean, too. To remember that moment at the bottom of the ocean where he'd taken root in her subconscious at an all-consuming level.

He growled, and pulled her against his torso, his arms so strong she lost her breath all over again. His erection pushed hard into her hip.

That warm flicker of lust pooled low in her belly. She would take Zac any way she could have him, but the niggling thought needed an answer.

"How long can you stay?" she breathed.

"As long as you'll let me."

Her eyebrows pinched together. "Who's taking care of your grandmother?"

His posture slumped slightly. "Jordan, can we sit?"

"Sure." She led him to her sofa, waiting for his reply.

"Gram passed . . . shortly after you left."

Her hands flew over her mouth. "No. Zac, I am so sorry."

His eyes grew watery. "It was peaceful. She was happy. Drifted off in her sleep, no pain."

She grabbed his hands. He'd been dealing with this all the last month by himself. She couldn't imagine his torture. "I'm so, so sorry. I know how much she meant to you."

"I miss her every day, but I miss you, too," he tightened his grip. "I want to *stop* missing. Jordan, I'll do whatever it takes to be with you. I'll rent the place out, and move up here, if you'll have me."

Her chest swelled. "If I'll have you? Of course, I will!" A tear chased another down her cheek. Tears of sadness over Eva, and even more of utter joy at the man before her.

He pointed with his chin. "Aren't you going to open your gift?"

"You are the gift." She pressed an urgent kiss on his lips. Nothing could make her happier than this man.

He kissed her back, then pulled away. "Trust me. This one is sparklier." He set the package on her lap. "Please."

She ripped open the brown paper to reveal bubble wrap held together with tape. She pulled it apart with Zac's help.

Jordan sucked in a breath.

Light glinted off the glass wave she'd admired in the shop. Her favorite piece.

"Oh God. It's beautiful. How did you know?"

"It was the first thing you touched when we walked in, and the last thing you smiled at on your way out. With our scuba trip, and the kiss we shared, I just knew."

Aside from Zac's smiling face at her front door, she'd never seen anything more beautiful. She set it back on the table.

"Thank you. I can't believe you bought it."

He gently touched the pendant at her neck. "You're wearing the flower necklace."

"I wear it every day. That was one of the best days of my life."

His lips curved upward.

She cupped his cheek. "Zac, I love you, and I missed you, too. I want to be with you."

She kissed him, slowly, sweetly . . . because how else would she know this was real? He was in San Francisco, sitting in her living room. Suddenly, the world was perfect.

"But why me?" he asked. "I haven't accomplished much of anything."

More kisses stopped the words from his mouth. "Why not you? You're the sweetest man I've ever met. Who loves with his whole heart. That's all I need. Besides, I'm not perfect by any means."

His eyes rounded. "You're not? That's a deal breaker for me, sorry." Then he grinned.

"I'm no picnic," she warned. "I'm stubborn, and a recovering perfectionist. Insatiable, and rarely quiet."

"Consider me informed. I'm looking forward to that insatiable part." He brushed her hair back. "While we're listing flaws, I'm a bit messy in the mornings, have an unhealthy relationship with tamales, and am fiercely loyal to the ones I love."

She laughed. "I'm counting on that last one. Any more you care to list?"

He pulled her feet across his lap. "Even though I've been stuck a million times, I can't stand needles. I like to be the one driving, and am notorious at giving directions." He narrowed his eyes. "And despite the run-in with Marco, I'm not the violent type."

Jordan grinned. "Can I tell you what *I* see?"

"Please, do."

She straddled his body, adjusting her hips to press into his groin. The heat and pressure were oh so welcome. "You're handsome, but don't flaunt it. Without even lifting a finger, everyone seems to like you. You make the most delicious mango margarita." She caressed his chin with the tip of her finger. "You love unconditionally with ease. And I crave the way you make me scream."

His hands moved up her back, slow and sensual. His dick lengthened against her core as if anticipating release. "That's a guilty pleasure of mine."

"Then you *are* perfect. You showed me how life's imperfections are the best parts. Things like my reaction to the cinnamon, and the hair on my body I can't stand, and not as pretty as other girls. You take me for who I am, flaws and all."

"What flaws? I wouldn't change a thing about you."

"Exactly." She kissed him again, longer. "I love you, Zac. So much it hurts. Hurts to be without you." She ground against his lap, giving in to the spontaneous physical pull.

"I'm so glad you opened the door," he breathed.

"I'm so glad you're here." She moved her lips over his, smooth and possessive, fusing them together.

His tongue plunged into her mouth as his fingers dug into her shoulders.

God, being in his embrace was as natural as breathing.

She snaked her arms around his neck, pressing closer.

He broke the kiss and whispered, "I love you, Jordan."

Her smile made her cheeks ache. She couldn't believe the love of her life, the man that had invaded her thoughts for weeks, was here in her apartment, holding her, saying those beautiful words. Setting her soul on fire.

She rose and offered a hand. "Come with me."

He accepted, his eyes twinkling with amusement.

As she made her way down the short hallway toward the bedroom, she stripped out of her shirt, and unbuttoned her shorts, dropping them on the wood floors. In the bedroom, she was only in her bra and panties.

"Wow. Nice view."

The double window overlooked a hill lined with pale, multicolored homes four stories tall. Her sheer slate-blue curtains framed the window with plenty of light. Ideal privacy.

She turned and sat on the edge of her queen-sized bed, the antique white iron headboard her favorite piece with fancy feather-like designs. Perfect for gripping onto.

"Nice bedroom, too." Zac grinned.

"Thanks. Plenty of room for both of us, don't ya think?"

He stepped into her embrace. "Perfect."

He gave her a sweet kiss that told her she'd made the right decision. She'd spent a month without him, and that's all it took to make her realize it was more than enough.

She yanked on his T-shirt, sliding her hands up his bare

torso and pushing his shirt off. She unfastened his shorts and pushed them with his briefs to the floor. His beautiful cock stood at attention.

With a flick of his wrist, he unclasped her bra and sent it flying. "I love a woman who knows what she wants."

She waggled her eyebrows as her fingers stroked his member from root to tip. "Can you handle it?" She tipped her head.

He pulled her to her feet, then grabbed her ass cheeks with his large warm hands. "Baby, I can handle anything you throw at me."

The wetness at the apex of her thighs grew. She ached to feel him inside her. Stepping backward to her bed, she slid her panties to the floor. "I have a condom in that drawer." She pointed to her nightstand.

He shook his head and bent down to his shorts. He fished out a condom from his pocket, and worked it over his impressive length.

"You came prepared." She lifted an eyebrow.

He lowered his body over hers, his warmth instantly radiating to her core. His cock nestled against her sex.

She moaned.

"Jordan, I carried this around for four weeks." Using his finger as a guide, he slowly pushed inside her. Her back bowed off the bed, and they both groaned. "I held out hope that you might walk back over that pool patio at the resort." He stroked her core causing her muscles to clench around him.

"Or do back handsprings on your beach?"

He claimed her mouth like a starving man devouring his last meal. "Baby." His panting came heavier. "You did back handsprings on my heart, and I've loved every moment."

His movements, every push and pull, brought her to the brink of ecstasy. "Oh God, Zac." An orgasm rippled through her in a slow, heated roll of pleasure.

Zac pumped harder, calling out her name in his own release. He rolled to the side, pulling her into him.

"God, I can't believe you're here."

His smile lit up the room. "Believe it."

"And you'll stay with me." No way would she have this man living anywhere else. She wanted him all to herself.

"If you'll have me, *querida*."

"Oh crap," she exclaimed. She jumped off the bed.

He pushed onto his elbows. "What are you doing?"

"Throwing out the cinnamon."

"Now?" His voice hitched higher.

"Baby, if you don't like, you'll just have to chase me," she said, giving him a sassy wiggle of her ass.

The wicked glimmer in his eyes and the sexy-as-hell smile were the last things she saw before she ran out of the room.

*But wait! There's more! Check out **Cold Spell** and read all about Liddy.*

Chapter 1

THE RAIN SLAPPED against Liddy's apartment window, fitting her mood. Dark, dreary, unwelcome, with no end in sight.

San Francisco's five straight days of rain made the whole city dismal. Meteorologists predicted at least three more.

Ugh. Was *ugh* a mood? Because if so, that was her mantra the last week.

Everything was constantly wet. She'd step into work at the designer boutique shop, and have wet shoes all day and matted hair. She'd come home, strip out of her wet clothes, and veg in front of the TV. *God bless sweatpants!*

When will this rain ever end?

Every northern California resident who lived there any significant amount of time, knew rainy season started in November. So, she shouldn't be surprised. Didn't mean she didn't like it any less. *Ugh.*

She shot a return text her friend, Sam, who asked if she could borrow her black mini Coach handbag for some event she and Chase had that Sunday.

Sure. She didn't need it.

She had no plans to go out. No boyfriend to make plans with. Just that morning she questioned if she was even capable of love.

How can a thirty-year old, modern, successful woman not have a man?

Jordan, her other best friend, called the other day inviting her to the grand opening of the new scuba shop her boyfriend Zac and his business partner were opening that weekend. *Mar Profundo USA* was to be the best new dive shop in town.

Liddy wouldn't miss it. But it wouldn't be as enjoyable flying solo.

Shit! She needed to break out of this gloomy funk.

When the hell was their next vacation? For the past two years, she and her besties escaped the daily grind on a week-long vacation, usually someplace warm and sunny. Both times, they'd found love.

Liddy'd found a beach snow globe on their last trip that read *Puerto Vallarta* across the bottom. She had to get it—snow over a sandy beach in Mexico.

"Ha," she said to the empty space, staring at the snow globe on the windowsill over her kitchen sink.

Maybe I should get a cat.

Oh God, did she just think that?

No, she needed a change of scenery. Her boss told her

to take some vacation before the holiday season got crazy.

She turned on the stove to heat water for tea.

That was the answer. Their last vacation was over a year and half ago. Time to get the heck out of town. And nowhere *near* Mexico this time.

She reached for her phone. "Jordan."

"Hey, *chica*. What's up?" The sound of creaking trampolines and pounding vaults thundered in the background. The gymnastics coach should be finished with her high school team practice by now.

"J, sorry. I thought practice would be over."

"It's okay. We're wrapping up."

"K. So, what's the chance, after opening weekend, you, me, and Sam can go on vacation?"

"Um, pretty good for me. School's out the whole week of Thanksgiving. Does that work?"

"Hell, yes. I'm sick and tired of the rain. Ya know what else?"

"I know, you're sick and tired of being sick and tired."

"Damn straight." They chuckled together.

"Okay, I'll do some digging. How do you feel about snow skiing?"

She bit her lip. "I would love to, but that's a bit out of my price range. Hotel *and* lift passes..."

"Oh, don't worry about that. Zac's cousin works at a ski resort in Colorado, and can get us lift tickets. Which is why I thought of it."

"Fabulous! I'll call Sam."

She disconnected the line and punched Sam's preset button. Liddy's heart rate kicked up.

"Samantha Louise Callahan, soon to be Bradshaw," she announced when Sam picked up.

"Lydia Michelle Drake," her friend countered playfully.

"I need a vacation."

"Oh, God. Me too. This wedding stuff is making me cross-eyed."

"Jordan's looking into a skiing trip. You up for it?"

"Long overdue. I'm in!"

"Super. I'll let you know when I hear from J."

Liddy set down her phone and poured the hot water over her tea bag. Suddenly, she could breathe a little easier. The rain lashing at her window didn't matter as much anymore either. She was leaving town.

Oh yeah.

A Message FROM THE AUTHORS

Thank you so much for reading!

If you enjoyed this story, please consider posting a review at one or more of your favorite retailers, as well as GoodReads. Even a short review, one or two lines, can be a tremendous help and encouragement to the authors. Your review is also a gift to other readers who may be searching for just this sort of story, and will be grateful you helped them find it.

Thank you!

Mia London & Susan Sheehey

About THE AUTHORS

Mia London

Mia London loves to write.

After reading fiction for years, she decided it was finally time to put those images and scenes floating around in her head down on paper.

She is a huge fan of romance, highly optimistic, and wildly faithful to the HEA (happily ever after). Her goal is to create a fantasy you will enjoy with characters you could love.

She lives in Texas with her attentive, loving, supermodel husband, and perfectly behaved, brilliant children. Her produce never wilts, there are no weeds in her flowerbeds, and chocolate is her favorite food group.

www.Facebook.com/MiaLondonAuthor
Twitter- @MiaLondonAuthor
Webpage- www.MiaLondon.com
Email- mia@mialondon.com

Susan Sheehey writes contemporary romance and romantic suspense adventure. Water plays a crucial element in all her novels, and she's a strong advocate for Autism awareness and acceptance. She squeezes in writing time between chauffeuring around her two boys, and guzzling down French Vanilla coffee. Her beloved husband keeps her relatively sane, and full of laughter. She and her family live in Texas.

www.SusanSheehey.com
www.Facebook.com/SusanSheehey
www.Twitter.com/SusieQWriter
www.Pinterest.com/SusanSheehey

Join her newsletter for monthly announcements, updates, ARC requests, and special giveaways!

https://landing.mailerlite.com/webforms/landing/p5b0i9

Interested in reading Advance Reader Copies of Susan's upcoming novels? Let her know here:
https://susansheehey.com/contact/